She approached him and reached out to touch his scar, running her index finger along the pale line.

She was painstakingly gentle, and it made him want to kiss her. They were standing so close he could've leaned forward and captured her mouth with his. But he didn't take the liberty. They stared at each other instead, steeped in a strange kind of intimacy.

"I'm glad you survived the accident," Carol said, smoothing his hair across his brow.

"So am I." But before things got unbearably awkward, Jake stepped back, trying to restrain the tenderness between them. "After the crash, I used to pray to Uncta, a deity from Choctaw mythology who steals fire from the sun. I was the only one who was rescued from the car before it went up in flames."

"Did you think Uncta had saved you?"

"No, but I wanted to steal fire, too. To have his powers."

But that wasn't going to help Jake now. He'd already jumped straight from the frying pan and into the flame, feeling things for Carol that he wished he didn't feel. He still wanted to kiss her, as hot and passionately as he could.

* * *

Waking up with the Boss is part of the Billionaire Brothers Club trilogy—Three foster brothers grow up, get rich...and find the perfect woman.

Dear Reader,

Where is the most exotic place you've ever been? For me, it's the trip I took while writing this book. It wasn't a real holiday, where I got to pack my suitcases and board a boat or a plane. But it was a journey just the same. As you'll soon discover, Jake Waters, the billionaire hero of this story, whisks Carol Lawrence, his loyal assistant, off to a private island in the Caribbean. And that's the trip I took, too, deep in my mind.

I created the island and everything on it. I set the stage for the party they were scheduled to attend. I built the mansion where they were staying. I imagined the mermaid they shaped and formed from mounds of wet sand. I cooked the gourmet food they ate. I encouraged them to dance, to sip champagne, to enjoy the magical feel of each other.

And in the midst of the story, I watched them fall wonderfully in love.

So you see, the most exotic place you've ever been can be part of a book or a movie or a song. It can be a place someone else created in his or her mind. Or a place that you'd always dreamed about, anywhere in the world, real or imaginary.

Even inside the pages of a sweet and sexy romance novel called *Waking Up with the Boss*.

Love and hugs,

Sheri WhiteFeather

SHERI WHITEFEATHER

WAKING UP WITH THE BOSS

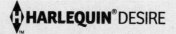

Recycling programs
for this product may
not exist in your area.

ISBN-13: 978-0-373-73479-5

Waking Up with the Boss

Printed in U.S.A.

Sheri WhiteFeather is an award-winning, bestselling author. She writes a variety of romance novels for Harlequin and is known for incorporating Native American elements into her stories. She has two grown children who are tribally enrolled members of the Muscogee Creek Nation. She lives in California and enjoys shopping in vintage stores and visiting art galleries and museums. Sheri loves to hear from her readers at sheriwhitefeather.com.

Books by Sheri WhiteFeather

Harlequin Desire

Marriage of Revenge
The Morning-After Proposal

Billionaire Brothers Club

Waking Up with the Boss

Harlequin Special Edition

Family Renewal

The Bachelor's Baby Dilemma
Lost and Found Husband
Lost and Found Father

Byrds of a Feather

The Texan's Future Bride

Harlequin Romantic Suspense

Imminent Affair
Protecting Their Baby

Visit her Author Profile page at Harlequin.com,
or sheriwhitefeather.com, for more titles.

One

Carol Lawrence stood in her boss's luxurious high-rise office, with a zillion things running through her mind. Being Jake Waters's personal assistant was a demanding job, with most of her duties centered on organizing his social life. No doubt about it, the jet-setting real estate mogul kept her on her toes. Not only did he travel for work, purchasing properties all over the globe, he was the consummate party boy, dashing off to exotic locations with models and actresses and whoever else struck his rich-guy fancy.

Jake sat on the corner of his desk and flung his jacket over his unused chair. As always, his shirtsleeves were rolled up, exposing the colorful tattoos on his arms, and his dark brown hair was in sexy disarray.

With his disheveled good looks and need for speed, he reminded her of James Dean, except that Jake was half-Choctaw, his mixed-blood heritage lending his features an uncommon beauty.

He certainly wasn't the type of man she should be attracted to. He was too wild for a practical girl like her. Carol spent her free time on a nice, quiet quilting hobby, whereas Jake raced sports cars as his outlet. To her that seemed like an especially reckless thing for him to do, given that his entire family had been killed in a car crash, sending him into foster care as a child. Carol had also lost her family and become a foster kid, as well. But they didn't know each other back then, and the tragedies they'd both suffered didn't make for good bedfellows.

Still, she often wondered what taming a man like Jake would involve. *Yeah, right.* If the glamorous beauties he dated couldn't pin him down, then a simple gal with tidy blond hair and a sensible nature would never fit the bill. Jake was a thirty-one-year-old billionaire who'd even made some crazy internet "Beefcake Bachelor" list as one of the sexiest single men in Southern California. Women chased him with a vengeance. Of course, some of them kept trying to fix him, with the assumption that he was damaged from the loss of his family, using his free-spirited lifestyle to hide the pain. Carol didn't doubt that was true. She knew the anguish that being orphaned could cause. But her coping mechanism was much gentler than his. Someday she longed to get married and have children of her own, recapturing the home and hearth she'd lost.

Jake glanced up and caught her gaze, and a fluttery sensation erupted in her stomach, something that happened far too often when she was in his presence.

Determined to maintain her composure, Carol focused on her job. "So," she said, "are you going to attend Lena's birthday celebration?" Lena was a pop star with a penchant for partying who ran in the same live-for-the-moment circle as Jake.

"Damn straight I'm going to go. She's my bud. I wouldn't miss her thirtieth bash." He laughed a little. "She'll probably be half-naked and dancing on table-tops."

"No doubt." Lena was known for her antics. Carol was the same age as Lena, but she couldn't imagine behaving that way. "Who will be attending the party with you?"

"Now that's where I'm having a bit of a problem. I don't have a date."

"I thought you were seeing Susanne Monroe." A long, leggy brunette who was recently divorced from a famous baseball player. Carol had seen her strutting around the office a few times in her tight-as-sin dresses, her stilettos clicking as she walked.

"We're not together anymore."

It was over already? "Who ended it?"

"She did." He shrugged off the breakup. "But I was just a rebound for her, anyway."

Carol shook her head, then glanced out the bank of

floor-to-ceiling windows, where a view of Wilshire Boulevard, with its busy Los Angeles cityscape, was spread out before them. She'd worked for Jake for two years, but she still hadn't gotten used to the parade of women who came in and out of his life.

She turned back to face him. "I'm sure you'll find a date for Lena's soiree. But for now, do you want me to RSVP for you and a plus-one? And notify your pilot to be on standby for that weekend?" The party was being held on a private island in the southeastern Caribbean Sea. Lena was pulling out all the stops, away from the prying eyes of the paparazzi.

"Yeah. Thanks. It's a couples-only theme, so I'm going to have to bring someone. Lena's latest song is called 'Couples Only,' and she always creates parties around her songs." Jake paused, then looked at Carol as if he'd just solved a strange little puzzle. "Here's an idea. You can be my plus-one. That would save me the trouble of finding another companion, and it would give you a great getaway."

Oh, my God. Carol white-knuckled her iPad, holding it against her chest. He was suggesting that she fly off to a tropical island to drink and dance and be merry with him? Sure, she traveled with him when it was necessary, but she'd never been expected to fill in as one of his dates. "You can't be serious."

"Of course I am. Or I wouldn't have said it."

"But I'm not part of your crowd. I wouldn't fit in."

"Yes, you would. You already know a lot of them."

"I know them in a professional sense."

"So now you can socialize with them, too."

The nervous sensation in her stomach swirled. "I can't." There was no way she could spend a weekend with Jake and his friends. "And with you being my employer, it wouldn't be proper."

"Really, Carol? You're going to use that as an excuse? I'm not proposing that we have a mad, passionate affair. The couples-only theme doesn't mean that we have to be a real couple. It's just a party."

"On a private island," she defended herself. "And I didn't think you were proposing anything." She knew better than to assume he was interested in her, and even if by some off chance he was, she wasn't foolish enough to jeopardize her job over it. "It doesn't seem right for us to go away together. It would be different if it was a business trip."

"So we'll call it a business trip."

Who was he trying to kid? "A party hosted by Lena Kent is more like monkey business."

He laughed. "That's true. But Lena isn't that bad. She donates a lot of money to my charity."

"I know how generous she is." Carol also knew how important the nonprofit organization he and his foster brothers had founded was to him. "But this isn't a charity gig. It's one of her nutty parties."

"Yeah, but just think of what a smashing time you'll have, sipping the most expensive champagne in the world and eating the most delicious food imaginable. Not to mention lounging around in your bathing suit, with the sea at your beck and call. We'll probably go

crabbing, too. I'll bet you've never done that before."
He stood, coming to his full height. "This would give
you the opportunity to expand your horizons and experience new things. It's crazy how reluctant you are
to let down your guard and have a good time."

"I'm not afraid of enjoying myself." She wasn't the
bore he was making her out to be. "I hang out with my
girlfriends. I haven't had a boyfriend in a while, but I
go on online dates." So far none of them had worked
out, but she was still trying to meet someone. "I'm just
cautious, that's all."

"Of what? People like me? Come on, Miss Proper
Employee, spend a recreational weekend with your big,
bad boss and his spoiled band of misfits."

"Are you actually daring me?"

"Hell, yes." He poured on the charm, being as in-
sistent as ever. "So what do you say? Are you game?"

She wished that his foster brothers were going to be
there. She felt safe around Garrett and Max, with how
cautious they always seemed, preferring to lead more
private lives. They'd grown up with Jake in the same
foster home and remained as close to him as anyone
could be. But they didn't socialize with Jake's party
crowd.

He moved forward and put his hands on her shoulders. "Come on, just do it. Jump headfirst and see
where you land."

Carol squeezed her eyes shut, as if she really were
diving off a cliff. *One...two...three.* She counted the
breaths that left her lungs, then opened her eyes and

looked straight into his, intending to decline the invitation. But somewhere in the insanity of the moment, of standing just inches from him, of absorbing the warmth of his touch, she heard herself say, "Okay, I'll do it. I'll go with you."

"That's my girl." Jake removed his hands from her shoulders and stepped back, leaving a silent gap between them.

Heaven help her. Had she actually agreed to this?

A sense of panic hit her, in more ways than one. Not only was she going to be stranded on a tropical island with her big, bad boss and his spoiled band of misfits, she was going to have to fuss over her clothes.

"I have no idea what I'm supposed to wear to the party," she said. She wore professional ensembles to work and comfy threads on her days off, but this was a whole other ball game.

He waved away her concern. "Just call Millie and have her bring a bunch of stuff to your house. Then pick whatever you want and have her bill me for it."

Millie was his stylist, a woman who also worked with celebrity clients. "You don't have to do that."

"I want to. Besides, you wouldn't be able to afford this type of couture on your own." He shot her a playful grin. "I'd have to give you a ridiculously huge raise."

She returned his smile. "Heaven forbid." In actuality, he already paid her a generous salary. But if he said the clothes were out of her price range, then she believed him. "I'll call her later today and see what her schedule is like." The party was less than a month away, and Carol wanted to be prepared. She never did anything last minute. "At least Millie already knows that I'm not a model or actress or Beverly Hills type. I could never wear anything straight off the runway. I have too much meat on my bones."

Automatically, his gaze traveled the length of her. "There's nothing wrong with having curves."

She could have kicked herself for drawing his attention to her shape. "I didn't mean it that way." She'd already learned to accept her fuller figure and stop trying to be skinnier than her body type allowed.

He kept checking her out, not overtly, but still looking, still being a guy. "Be sure to tell Millie to include beachwear," he said. "Just so you'll have a complete weekend wardrobe."

"That's fine." At this point, Carol wanted to hightail it out of his office. But she couldn't run off without wrapping things up. She hurriedly asked, "What sort of accommodations do they have on the island?"

"It's a mansion that Lena is renting. There are caretakers who live on the property, but she'll be hiring a full staff to run it like a hotel while we're there. When you RSVP, make sure to let her assistant know that we need two rooms. Otherwise, he'll assume that my plus-one will be staying with me."

"Yes, of course. I'll take care of it." After a beat of anxious energy, she said, "I better get back to work."

"You *are* working."

"I meant on something other than the arrangements for Lena's party. You have other commitments besides that." His calendar was filled with business dinners and charity events and city council meetings.

"I don't know what I'd do without you. You're good at keeping me organized."

"I'm just doing my job." But even so, this discussion seemed oddly personal. She hoped that she wasn't making a mistake by going to the Caribbean with him. How was she going sit beside him on the beach, wearing nothing but a swimsuit?

Just as she thought about the part of their trip when they'd be scantily clad, the sun shifted in the sky and the light from the windows spilled into the room, brighter than before.

He stood there for a moment, in the afternoon glare, looking as gorgeous as ever, before he picked up the remote from his desk and closed the blinds.

"I'll talk to you later," she said, telling herself not to worry, even if she could feel him watching her, much too closely, as she walked out the door.

Jake pulled his Gullwing Mercedes coupe, one of the many classic sports cars in his collection, into a guest parking spot at Carol's apartment. He didn't believe in letting his cars sit around, all pretty and polished and untouched. It didn't matter how rare or pricey they were, he drove the hell out of them. He treated women with the same reverence and vigor. But Carol wasn't his lover, and he had no business being here. Still, he'd decided to stop by because he knew that she was meeting with the stylist today. He figured the appointment was over by now. Of course, he'd timed it that way on purpose. He was curious to see what Carol had chosen.

He was curious about all sorts of things about her. Jake had been having some crazy fantasies about his assistant.

Carol was a fascinating woman, with a sinful body and modest values. An enigma, if there ever was one. And damn if her good-girl nature didn't turn him on. It was weird, too, because proper girls weren't his usual type. He'd never had the urge to pull someone into the fray, not the way he was doing with her.

Maybe it was because they shared similar backgrounds. Maybe that was why he was daring her to let down her guard and have a good time. Whatever the reason, he needed to curb his desire. He couldn't seduce her when they were on their trip. He absolutely, positively couldn't, no matter how tempting the thought was. Jake knew better than to cross that line with a woman who worked for him. Besides, she prided herself on being well-behaved and corrupting her would be wrong.

He glanced toward Carol's apartment. He'd never actually been inside her place before; he didn't make a habit of visiting his employees at their homes. He did own this building, though. It was one of his favorite properties. He gave her a discount on the rent, a perk that came with her job. But regardless of the deal they'd worked out, he wasn't her landlord, at least not directly. A management company ran the day-to-day operations and collected the rent.

Jake got out of the car and strode to Carol's door. She lived in a unit on the ground floor surrounded by foliage. Built in the 1930s, the complex boasted Spanish-style architecture and was within walking distance to restaurants, shopping centers and farmers' markets.

He rang the bell, and she answered the summons with a surprised expression.

"Jake? What are you doing here?"

"I just thought I'd check on how the fashion meeting unfolded." He gestured jokingly to his ensemble. "Not that I'm the epitome of style today." He was attired in a plain white T-shirt, jeans and scuffed leather boots. "These are snazzy, though." He removed his sunglasses. They were the pair she'd given him last Christmas, similar to the kind James Dean used to wear. They were even trademarked with the actor's name.

She looked him over. "In that getup, you really could be him."

"Oh, sure." He mocked the comparison, even if he was flattered by it. "Maybe I should get a Porsche like his, the one he smashed himself up in."

She sucked in her breath, as if the wind had just been knocked out of her. "You shouldn't say things like that."

"I was just goofing around." And being stupid, he supposed. He should've known that she wouldn't think his comment was funny. "It was a great car, a 550 Spyder that he was driving on his way to a race. That's a pretty good reason for me to get one."

She stared at him, unmoving, unblinking. "I'd prefer that you didn't."

He leaned against the doorjamb, trying to ease the tension.

"Are you going to invite me in to see your clothes?" For now, she was wearing shorts and a loose-fitting khaki shirt, with her strawberry blond hair fastened into a ponytail at her nape. He imagined undoing the clip and running his hands through it. She had the silkiest-looking hair, with each piece always falling into place. Not that he should be thinking about messing up her hair. He was supposed to be keeping those types of thoughts in check.

"Yes, come on in." She stepped back to allow him entrance. The brightly lit interior featured hardwood floors and attractive window treatments. She'd decorated with art deco furnishings from the era of the building, mixed with crafty doodads. He noticed a patchwork quilt draped over the sofa. He knew she liked to sew. Sometimes she gave the quilts she made to the other women in the office, for birthdays and whatnot.

"You've done a nice job with the place," he said.

"Thank you." She had yet to relax. She still seemed bothered by what he'd said earlier.

Now he wished he could take it back. Not his interest in the Porsche, but the way he'd joked about it. He hooked his sunglasses into the V of his shirt, and she frowned at him.

"Do you race cars because you have a death wish?" she asked, rather pointedly.

Cripes, he thought. She had it all wrong. "I do it to

feel alive." Everything he did was for that reason. "I don't want to look back and regret anything."

"I hope that's the case."

"Believe me, it is." After waiting for the smoke to clear, he gestured to the quilt. "When I was a kid, we had one sort of like that hanging on our living room wall that my paternal grandmother made."

Carol inched closer to him. "You did?"

He nodded. "She died before I was born, but the design was associated with her clan."

"Do you still have it, tucked away somewhere?"

He shook his head. "It disappeared when I went into foster care. It was sold, I suppose. Or given away, or whatever else happened to my family's belongings." He glanced at the fireplace mantel, where he spotted a framed photograph of what he assumed was her family: three towheaded girls and a forty-something mom and dad, posing in a park.

He picked up the picture and quietly asked, "Are you in this?"

"Yes," she replied, just as softly. "I'm the older sister. I was about ten there."

He studied the image. Everyone looked happy. Normal. Like his family had been. But he didn't keep photos around. He couldn't bear to see them every day.

Jake was lucky that he'd bonded with Garrett and Max. They'd been a trio of troubled boys in foster care who'd formed a pact, vowing to get powerfully rich and help one another along the way. The goal had ultimately allowed them to become the successful men they were today. Without Garrett and Max, Jake would've wanted to die, for sure.

He wondered if anyone had helped Carol get through her grief or if she'd done it on her own. They rarely talked about their pasts. Jake didn't like revisiting old ghosts, his or anyone else's, but he was doing it with her now.

"It's a nice picture," he said, placing it back on the mantel. "It must have been a good day."

"It definitely was. It was taken at my dad's company picnic." Her voice remained soft, loving. "We all had a great time that day, especially my sisters. They were only a year apart and were really close. Sometimes people mistook them for twins, and they always got a kick out of that."

"I had two sisters, too. Only, they were older. I was their pesky little brother."

Her light green eyes locked on to his. "How old were you when…?"

"Twelve. How old were you?"

She let out her breath. "Eleven."

His heart dropped to his stomach. He knew that her family had died from carbon monoxide poisoning from a faulty appliance in their home. But he didn't know the details. "How did you survive when the rest of them didn't?"

"I wasn't there. I was at a neighbor's house. It was my first slumber party. I was younger than some of the other girls, so my parents were hesitant to let me go, but I begged them, so they gave in." She breathed a little deeper. "Not being home that night saved my life."

"It was different for me. I was in the car when it crashed. The impact was fast, brutally quick, but I remember it in slow motion." It had been like an out of body experience that never ended. "I have a scar." He pushed back the pieces of hair that fell across his forehead. "Here, just below my hairline. It was noticeable when I was young, but it's faded over the years."

She approached him and reached out to touch the scar, running her index finger along the pale line. She was painstakingly gentle, and it made him want to kiss her. They were standing so close he could've leaned forward and captured her mouth with his. But he didn't take the liberty. They stared at each other instead, steeped in a strange kind of intimacy.

"I'm glad you survived the accident," Carol said, smoothing his hair across his brow.

"So am I." But before things got unbearably awkward, Jake stepped back, trying to restrain the tenderness between them. "After the crash, I used to pray to Uncta, a deity from Choctaw mythology who steals fire from the sun. I was the only one who was rescued from the car before it went up in flames."

"Did you think Uncta had saved you?"

"No, but I wanted to steal fire, too. To have his powers."

But that wasn't going to help Jake now. He'd already

jumped straight from the frying pan and into the flame, feeling things for Carol that he wished he didn't feel. He still wanted to kiss her, as passionately as he could.

Two

Carol wondered what had gotten into her, touching Jake the way she had. She shouldn't have traced his scar or tried to subdue the unruly strands of his hair. Those types of things were reserved for lovers, not your boss.

But she wasn't going to apologize. That would only draw attention to what she'd done. She could already feel the discomfort it had caused.

Breaking the silence, she said, "I'll go get my new clothes so you can see them." It was the purpose of his visit, after all. But she wasn't going to offer to model them for him. That would be way too weird.

Carol dashed into her room and grabbed the garments.

She returned to the living room and laid them out

on her couch. She went back for the accessories, and then lined them up on the coffee table.

"That's a cool bounty," he said.

Yes, it was, with at least two different outfits per day, along with shoes, purses and beach bags to match. "I have you to thank for it."

"As long as you're happy with everything." He reached for a hanger with a flowing fabric draped around it. "What's this?"

"That's my party dress. It's a sarong." It was made from the finest silk in the world, decorated with a hand-painted design and trimmed in shiny glass beads.

"The material is beautiful, but how does it work?"

"There are lots of different ways to wrap it. Millie showed me how she thinks it will best suit me. This goes with it." She grabbed a big sheer scarf and swished it back and forth. "It's called a body veil. It goes around the dress for a fluttery effect."

"A body veil." He spoke softly. "That even sounds pretty."

She forged ahead. "Both pieces are from a Brazilian designer who just exploded onto the scene." She'd already memorized his name in case anyone at the party asked who she was wearing. "Millie said that they don't use beach towels in Rio. Instead, they lay a sarong in the sand and the women use them as cover-ups, too. But you probably already know that since you go there every year for Carnival."

Before she envisioned him doing wicked things in the streets of Rio, she quickly added, "My outfit was created as an evening gown and is much fancier than the sarongs they use at the beach. It's from the designer's most recent collection and hasn't even hit the stores yet. So I was wrong about not wearing something straight off the runway."

Jake put down the dress, treating it gently. "It has a romantic quality."

She supposed it did, especially with the inclusion of the body veil, but dang if she could come up with an appropriate response.

Was Jake as attracted to her as she was to him? Was that even possible? It was sure starting to feel like it.

He was now eyeing her new bikini. It wasn't an itty-bitty, stringy thing, but the design was nonetheless sexy. Millie had talked her into it, saying that the low-cut top and high-waist bottoms showed off her curves. Thankfully, Carol already had a bit of a tan from hanging out at the pool. It wasn't summer yet. It was still spring, when the Southern California weather varied from day to day, so sometimes she cheated and used a tanning bed at the salon, preparing for the hotter months ahead. However, she was cautious about not overdoing any type of UV exposure. She never did anything in excess.

Jake did, though. He was the king of indulgences. She couldn't imagine two people being more opposite, aside from the loss of their families, which had been their tie from the beginning. She'd first met him when she'd applied for a job at his Caring for Fosters Foundation, the organization he, Garrett and Max had cre-

ated that provided financial and emotional support to
foster children. She hadn't gotten the job, as her experience in nonprofits was limited. But Jake had made it
up to her, offering to hire her as his personal assistant,
a position that was also up for grabs at the time. And
now, here she was, two years later, trapped in feelings
she couldn't quite define.

"I should put everything back," she said. She wanted
that bathing suit out of sight, out of mind. Which was
foolish, she knew, considering that eventually he was
going to see her in it.

"I can help."

"That's okay, you don't have to."

"Really, I don't mind."

"All right." Carol gave in. Otherwise, letting him
handle her belongings might seem like a bigger deal
than it was, even if it was making her nervous.

With both of their arms full, he followed her down
the hall. They entered her room, and she placed her
load on the bed.

He followed suit, then said, "It's girlie in here."

"I guess it is, to some degree." Along with textured
wood furnishings, the decor consisted of dried flowers, lacy pillows and a tufted headboard upholstered in
blue velvet. "But what can I say?" She made a goofy
joke. "I hit like a girl, too. So you better watch out."

He laughed. "There's no such thing as hitting like
a girl. My sisters used to pummel the crap out of me.
But most of the time, I had it coming."

She teased him. "You were a troublemaker even then?"

"I used to embarrass them in front of their dates, telling the guys stupid things about them."

She kept up the banter. "Remind me not to have you around when I go on my next date."

His expression sobered. "I wouldn't do that to you, Carol. I'm not a kid anymore."

Boy, didn't she know it. He was about as grown-up as a man could get, tall and strong, with the deepest, darkest brown eyes. When he smiled, they twinkled, but when he was being serious, like now, those eyes could pierce a part of your soul.

Anxious to get him out of her room and back to neutral ground, she said, "I never even offered you anything."

He raised his eyebrows. "Anything?"

"A refreshment." She knew that he favored seltzer water, with ice and a twist of lemon. She did, too, a habit she'd picked up from him.

"A refreshment? Who says things like that?" A smile returned to his face. "Except for those old TV sitcom housewives. All you need is a ruffled apron to complete the picture."

"Smarty." She shrugged it off. "Maybe I was born in the wrong era."

"Maybe I was, too. Only, I would be a greaser." He slipped on his sunglasses, peering at her from beneath the tinted glass like a rabble-rouser. "Me and my fast cars."

She'd never been to one of his races, but she'd gotten used to knowing where he went, who he socialized with, even which women he took to bed.

Was it any wonder she was antsy about him being in her room? She'd spent far too much time beneath her covers thinking about the hot and sexy things his lovers sometimes said about him. One overzealous starlet had even blogged about her naughty escapades with him. Of course, he wasn't the only playboy who'd rung this woman's bell or who'd been mentioned in the blog. But he was the only one Carol cared about.

"So, do you want something to drink?" she asked.

He removed the glasses. "Sure."

They went into the kitchen, and she poured the drinks. When they returned to the living room, she was still fighting her wayward thoughts.

She just hoped that she was able to relax and enjoy herself on their trip, without her fantasies going wild. Because there was nothing tame about the battle raging inside her or how badly she needed to contain it.

Time went by in a busy blur, and now Jake was sitting beside Carol on his private jet, en route to the Caribbean. Normally he slept on long flights, shutting out the boredom, but he was wide-awake on this journey, fascinated by every move his traveling companion made.

With her reddish blond hair falling against her summer-white blouse, she looked soft and pretty, framed by the intermittent clouds billowing past her window. She'd been peering out the glass for a while, gazing at the ocean.

Finally, she turned back to him. She wasn't a frantic flyer. But she wasn't as comfortable in the air as he was, either. The aircraft was too big to land on the private island where they were going, so they'd be landing on another island, then taking a helicopter to their final destination.

"I researched the Caribbean," she said.

"You did?" He leaned a little closer, getting a deeper whiff of the fragrance she wore. It smelled crisp and fresh, like grapefruit, mixed with summer greens. "For what kind of information?"

"All kinds." She exaggerated a shiver. "You should have seen the snakes and spiders and scorpions I uncovered. Luckily our island doesn't have any of those things, at least not poisonous ones. No crocodiles, either."

He shifted in his seat. "Did you think Lena would choose a location with all that?"

"I just wanted to be sure. I didn't want to get bitten by some scary creature."

If he could get away with sinking his teeth into her, he would do it. "We're going to be fine."

"I packed a first-aid kit, just in case. We still need to watch out for jellyfish and things like that."

The only safety precaution Jake ever packed was condoms. Of course he'd skipped them this trip since it wasn't going to be a romantic adventure. Then again, he probably had some stored away in the side zipper compartment of his luggage, where he normally kept them. But none of that mattered since he and Carol weren't going to be together. Nor should he even be thinking about it.

"Speaking of scary creatures," she said.

He snapped back to attention. "What?"

"You have lots of strange beings on you."

He glanced down. Clearly she was talking about his tattoos.

She gestured to his right arm, which was the one closest to her. "What's the spidery-looking thing in the middle?"

"That's a depiction of Uncta."

"The deity who steals fire?"

Jake nodded. "And he is a spider, of sorts. He was able to appear in both human form and as a giant bronze spider. In his human form, he would entertain in his big fancy lair and offer advice to his guests. He told prophecies, too."

She gave Uncta's image a tentative touch, using the very tips of her nails. "I wonder what advice he would give you." She followed the lines of the drawing. "Or prophecies."

"I don't know." Jake wished her fingers on his flesh didn't feel so damned good. He imagined her clawing his back with those neatly manicured nails.

She moved on to another one of his tattoos: a beautiful young woman draped in a white gown, her long black hair blowing in the wind. "Is she a deity, too?"

"Yes." He tried to focus on his answer, instead of

how Carol was making him feel. "Her father is the god of the sun and her mother is the goddess of the moon."

"And what's her specialty?"

"She introduced corn to the people, providing the first seeds that led to the first harvest. Even today, she still wanders through cornfields, blessing the crops, looking like an angel from above. Or so the legend goes."

"And who is this?" Another question. Another touch.

One by one, he explained who each of the deities on his arms were. The two gigantic birds that created lightning and thunder. The hunting god who taught wolves how to howl. The female ruler of the swamplands who provided vegetation that was safe to use for medicine. Overall, he had ten mythical beings tattooed on his body, each with their own purpose. Carol seemed particularly fascinated with the human grasshopper goddess who ruled a subterranean world known as an earth-womb.

"She's the mother of the unliving," Jake said. "Not the dead, but the spirits who are waiting to be born."

"What's her name?"

"Eskeilay."

Carol repeated it, using the same rhythmic inflection he'd used. Then she asked, "Do you think your future children are with her, waiting to emerge?"

Jake shot her an incredulous look. "Seriously? Can you see me being a dad? There's no way I'm ever having kids."

"I suppose it was a silly question." She smiled like

an imp. "But it seems like a waste of Eskeilay's powers, to just sit there on your arm in her bendy grasshopper pose, with her antennae poking out of her head, with no little Jacob Waters babies floating around."

"Listen to you, being funny." He rubbed the spot where Eskeilay was. It was starting to tingle, almost as if the goddess was coming to life. "It wasn't like that in the beginning. The first spirits waiting to be born weren't babies. They were just people, living in Eskeilay's world. But when it got too overcrowded, they evacuated, and on their way to earth, they accidentally trampled some grasshoppers, including Eskeilay's own mother. Needless to say, she was pissed. So the opening to earth was blocked, and the rest of the people trapped underground were turned into ants."

"Oh, that's just great. Now whenever I see an ant, I'm going to think of that."

"Sorry. But you know how mythology is. Something disturbing always happens. But in this case, it also explains how ants came to be and why they live in holes in the ground," he explained. "These stories are based on what I was told. There are other Choctaw myths that don't coincide with what I was taught. But that's common with folklore. Stories are apt to change, depending on who tells them, and my dad liked to put his own spin on them. Sometimes my mom even got in on it, adding little details." He paused in remembrance. "Mom was a blue-eyed blonde with French and English ancestry, but she used to joke around and say that was she part Choctaw. Or that she had been for nine months when she was pregnant with us kids. And that's what gave her the right to horn in on those stories."

Carol smiled. "That's cute."

"My dad thought so, too. They were this ridiculously happy couple. I used to think I was lucky because they didn't scream and fight like some of my friends' parents. Or they weren't getting divorced or whatever. Then they ended up gone in the worst possible way."

"I know just how you feel." She fell silent, her gaze locking on to his. Then she said, "Except that I want to get married and have children someday. That's really important to me."

"I figured as much." She struck him as the wifely sort. "You seem like you need all that homeyness. But I don't. For me, it's easier to be unencumbered."

"Yes, I can tell."

He glanced away, his thoughts slipping back in time once again. "My sisters used to talk about the kinds of weddings they wanted to have." He frowned, his dead siblings' broken dreams burrowing uncomfortably in his brain. "They went on and on about how romantic it was going to be. But I suppose it's common for teenage girls to do that."

She heaved a heavy breath. "I can't even tell you how many times I thought about it when I was young, even before I was a teenager."

He envisioned her, a lonely little girl in foster care, longing for the big day. It made him want to comfort her, to make the child she'd once been feel better. But it made him want to pull away from her, too.

But even so, he asked, "What kind of men do you date?"

She sat a little more upright. "What type do you think?"

"Oh, I don't know." He turned cavalier. "Big hairy bikers?"

She rolled her eyes. "Come on, Jake. I'm being serious."

In spite of his joke, he wasn't feeling particularly humorous, either. "Okay, then how about nice, proper guys who would make good husbands?"

She folded her hands on her lap. All she needed was a pair of tidy white gloves to complete the ladylike picture.

"Exactly," she said.

Yes, he thought. *Exactly.* He already knew the answer before he'd posed the question. And now that she was being so prim and marriage-minded, all he wanted to do was get to the island and sweep her into the debauchery that had become his life.

Where nice, proper guys didn't exist.

Three

It was breathtaking, Carol thought. The mansion where she and Jake and the rest of the partygoers were staying was a sprawling French Colonial–style estate, amid a gorgeous sandy white beach.

The caretakers, an older couple local to the area, escorted Carol and Jake to their rooms. Lena had brought the rest of the staff over from the States, along with a beauty team to provide in-room makeup, hair and nail services to her guests. Massage therapists could be had, as well.

No one had seen Lena yet. She wouldn't be making an appearance until the party. But she was the type who liked to make a grand entrance, so Carol wasn't surprised.

Carol's and Jake's rooms were located on the second floor and were next to each other, with adjoining doors in the center. For now they were open, making it one huge suite.

"We're going to have to lock those as soon as we get settled in," she said.

"We will," he replied, going onto his veranda.

Carol's balcony had the same view. But she joined him on his, standing beside him on the airy structure. Beyond the oasis-style pool was the ocean. In another direction, she spotted a mountainous terrain, surrounding a lush green glimpse of rain forest.

She thought it would be a wonderful setting for a destination wedding. The caretakers had already given them a bit of history on the custom-built mansion, which could be rented out for weddings. Not that she should be thinking about that. But after the discussion she and Jake had had on the plane, her mind was still immersed in marriage.

"It's beautiful here," she said as a breeze stirred between them.

Jake turned toward her. "You're not afraid of getting bitten by something scary anymore?"

"I already told you they don't have superscary things on this island." Except for him, she thought. The look in his soul-stealing eyes was filled with danger. Or lust. Or something she was too chicken to identify. He was actually giving her goose bumps.

He kept staring at her, and she crossed her arms to ward off the sexy chill.

Trying to stay focused on their schedule, she told him, "The caretakers said that the chef was making seafood for dinner, with lots of vegan dishes on the side for the people who prefer that." Their meals would be served in their rooms. After that, they could rest before they got ready for the party, which was scheduled for later that night.

He kept looking at her. "I'm getting a little hungry. Are you?"

She nodded. She definitely wanted to keep her mouth busy. But she didn't have to wait for the meal. Baskets of fruit and nuts and other snacks had already been provided, along with fully stocked portable bars. A glass of wine sounded good about now. But Carol would be indulging in alcohol at the party, so she figured it was best to wait until then.

"Before I forget, I have something for you," he said. "I'll go get it."

She remained on the veranda while he rummaged through his luggage. He returned with a trim white box.

She lifted the lid and uncovered an elegant gold bangle encrusted with round-cut diamonds surrounded by multicolored stones. There was also a pair of starfish-shaped earrings, also glittering with diamonds.

Her pulse quickened. "They're magnificent, Jake." The pieces were going to look stunning with her dress. "Are they on loan?" She knew that jewelers sometimes let their rich and famous clients borrow from their inventory.

"No. I paid for them."

Oh, my. "You shouldn't have done that."

"I wanted to. Besides, I checked with Millie to see if you'd gotten any jewelry to go with your outfit, and she said that you hadn't."

"I didn't want to go overboard and spend more than was necessary." She gazed at the gems. "But this is way too much. I should return them to you after the party."

"Seriously? That doesn't make any sense. They were purchased to complement your wardrobe, and you're keeping the clothes. So why would you give the earrings and bracelet back? They're just part of the mix."

She studied each piece again. "They really are amazing."

"Don't be too impressed. I had Millie tell me what to get. I'm not good at giving women gifts."

That was true. Sometimes he even relied on Carol to decide on what type of flowers to send to his lovers. But she shouldn't have used that as a comparison, not with the way he was making her feel.

Had she made a mistake, coming on this trip with him? It was certainly the most impetuous thing she'd ever done.

She closed the box and held it against her chest, where her heart was thumping much too madly. She liked being in his company, far more than she should.

"So it's settled then?" he asked. "You're keeping the jewelry?"

"Yes, thank you. I'll accept it." What good would it do to argue the point, when she was already losing ground?

"I should go unpack now," she said.

He gestured to the pool. "Maybe I'll go for a quick swim before the food gets here."

She didn't want to think about him diving into the water in nothing but a bathing suit, but her imagination went haywire just the same. No doubt his naturally bronzed body would be a sight to behold.

Attempting to make a graceful exit, she said, "I'll see you when it's time for the party."

"I'll see you, too."

He didn't turn away and neither did she. They just stood there, immersed in each other. So much for a graceful exit.

Finally, she ended the connection and headed to her room, closing and locking the door on her side that separated their living quarters. She heard him close the door on his side, too, and turn the bolt.

Carol breathed a heavy sigh of relief, then glanced around at the glamorous antique furnishings and four-poster bed. Jake's room more or less mimicked hers, which didn't make it any easier, knowing he was on the other end of those adjoining doors.

She warned herself to stay away from her veranda in case he did go for a swim. Fantasizing about him was bad enough. She didn't need to watch him and become a voyeur, too.

As the evening progressed, Jake was more than ready to blow off some steam. After his swim, he'd eaten dinner. Then he'd fallen asleep, rumpled and naked. From there, he'd dragged his ass out of bed and taken a long, hot shower.

And now he was standing in front of the mirror in a designer suit, his hair styled in its usual way.

If he knew Carol, she'd probably been ready for hours. His assistant was an early bird, whereas Jake waited right up to the end to dash off to wherever he was going.

As if on cue, his phone beeped with a text. No doubt it was Carol, telling him it was time to leave. She always sent him reminders for everything.

He checked. Sure enough it was her. They agreed to meet in the hallway, outside their rooms.

She got there first, and as soon as Jake saw her, he marveled at her beauty. Her dress was wrapped in a stylish yet sultry way, complementing her voluptuous figure. It wouldn't take much to untie the sarong, either. A pull here, a tug there. The body veil that went with it was incorporated into the design, flowing softly, making her ensemble even sexier.

Her makeup was light and elegant, and her shoulder-length, blunt-cut hair was straight and shiny. The starfish earrings twinkled next to her face, and the bracelet shone at her wrist. Her skin had just the slightest hint of shimmer, too, especially around the swell of her cleavage. Or maybe that was where he noticed it most. He assumed it was from some sort of glittery lotion. Her strappy evening bag was small and delicate—the kind women carried when they danced.

"You look hot," he said. He stepped back to take

another admiring glance. "Seriously, you could be a siren who roams the island, tempting guys like me to come out to play."

She flushed accordingly. "Thank you. But I'm not trying to tempt anyone, and you're always ready to play with some pretty young thing."

Not the way he wanted to play with her. "Don't worry. Tonight I'm going to be good."

Her gaze roamed over him. "Then I guess it's all right to tell you that you look rather hot yourself?"

Hell, yes, it was all right. He liked being in her sights, even if nothing was going to happen between them. "Millie brought a bunch of stuff to my house, too, and this is what I picked." Suddenly he realized his shirt was the same minty green color as Carol's eyes. He hadn't chosen it for that reason, at least not deliberately. But who knew what tricks his attraction to her was playing on his subconscious?

"Are you ready?" he asked.

"As ready as I'm ever going to be."

Was she still worried about fitting in with his crowd?

"Just hold on tight and have a good time."

"Hold on to what?"

"Me." He took her hand. "It's a couples-only theme, remember?"

She threaded her fingers through his. "I still can't believe I agreed to come here with you."

"It's too late to back out." He squeezed her hand. For now she was his plus-one, and he wasn't letting her go.

They took the staircase to the main ballroom on the

first floor. Already, they could hear the thumping base of music from a DJ's turntable.

The white-pillared ballroom exploded with color and flair. The couples-only theme was expressed in enormous paintings and life-size statues that had been commissioned specifically for the party, with depictions of legendary lovers, throughout the ages, entwined in a variety of emotional embraces.

A huge flat-screen monitor projected images that complemented the music, and scattered throughout the marble dance floor were gilded cages big enough for two, where couples could go inside and dance with each other. Jake thought it was intriguing. He didn't know if Carol would agree to do that with him, but it wouldn't hurt to ask when the moment felt right. It was just a bit of fun, after all. They were supposed to enjoy the festivities, and those cages were part of it.

The birthday girl wasn't there yet. Clearly, Lena wasn't quite ready to splash onto the scene and make her debut. Most of the guests had arrived and were partaking of food, drink and dance. A gourmet buffet offered lavish hors d'oeuvres and frothy desserts. Although Jake was still full from dinner, the pastries sure looked good.

"Good grief," Carol said. "This is something else."

Jake continued to hold her hand, giving her time to settle into the environment. A three-tiered fountain filled with ice was large enough to bathe in, with pink lemonade spilling from the spigots. Champagne was being served as well, delivered by waitstaff garbed in

French Colonial attire to match the mansion. There was a huge aquarium bar, too, stocked with angelfish and tended by bikini-clad bartenders wearing blue wigs and fluffy white wings. Indoor and outdoor tables were available, with figurine candles shaped into historic couples as the centerpieces. The party was an eclectic mix of whatever appealed to Lena's imagination.

After Jake and Carol took the champagne that was offered to them, she said, "I don't know where to begin."

"Anywhere you want."

She sipped her drink. "I think I'd like a pastry to go with this."

"That sounds good to me." He escorted her to the buffet and grabbed a treat for himself, too.

She wanted to eat outside, so they went onto the courtyard and sat with a few other couples who'd also decided to start their evening off outdoors. Jake introduced Carol to them. He knew most of the people in attendance.

While Carol chatted with Lena's songwriting partner and his wife, Jake studied the Napoleon and Josephine matchbooks that were on the table. The candle was a likeness of them, too, with their names scrolled across the bottom of the stand. He went ahead and struck a match and lit the wick. The wax emitted a rose scent.

Carol turned toward him, and they watched it burn together. Then she said, "Did you know that Josephine's birth name was Marie-Josèphe-Rose? And that she went by Rose until Napoleon started calling her Josephine?"

"No, I wasn't aware of that." But the rose scent was making a bigger impact now, getting stronger as the candle burned.

"She was born in the Caribbean on the island of Martinique. I came across references to that area when I was researching the islands around here, too."

He smiled. "And now we're sitting at Napoleon and Josephine's table, with you sharing your research with me."

She returned his smile. "Sometimes I overdo things like that."

"Yes, but what an interesting conversation it's turning out to be." He was fascinated by the details she'd provided. She looked beautiful in the candlelight, too, against the backdrop of sand and surf on the other side of the courtyard.

The songwriter interrupted, announcing to the entire group, "We should all go inside now. Lena will be appearing shortly."

"Do you know how she'll be making her entrance?" Jake asked.

"Yes, but she'd kill me if I spilled the beans." The other man took his wife's arm. "We'll see you in there."

"Sure." Jake wished he could stay where he was. He was enjoying being out here with Carol.

"I guess we better head in, too," she said after everyone else was gone.

"Yeah. I guess we better." They'd lingered long enough.

"Should we blow out Napoleon and Josephine?" she asked.

"You can do it."

She pursed her lips, and he watched her extinguish the flame, the candle's floral scent still drifting softly through the air.

Word got around that Lena was due to arrive, and the party buzzed with anticipation. Carol compared it to waiting for the stroke of midnight on New Year's Eve. Or a fireworks show on the Fourth of July.

Speaking of fireworks...

Jake stood beside her, his arm just barely grazing hers. She wanted to reach for his hand and hold it the way she'd done earlier, letting the excitement of touching him course through her veins. But she refrained.

Suddenly the blinds were closed on the French doors. A moment later, the chandeliers went out, the ballroom going pitch-black. Carol moved closer to Jake, not wanting to lose him in the dark.

When the lights returned, it was in the form of spinning strobes and black lights, creating shimmering effects and completely changing the atmosphere.

The DJ's clothing and equipment shone brightly. Clearly, he was part of the show. Carol held her breath as one of the cages began to ascend from the dance floor, its cylindrical base rising on a hydraulic platform above the crowd. A man and woman were inside it, standing like statues. Their skintight jumpsuits glowed with graffiti-type artwork. They also had fluorescent streaks in their hair and makeup that illuminated their faces.

The DJ announced the caged duo, and the crowd cheered and clapped. It was Lena and her current boyfriend, Mark, who was one of her backup dancers.

Lena's "Couples Only" song began to play, and more cheers and clapping erupted.

Lena and Mark danced, moving rhythmically in a magical performance. Along with everyone else, Carol was riveted by the way they interacted with each other. Jake stared up at them, too.

As the song ended, the cage was lowered back down to the ground. The door swung open and Lena and Mark emerged, rushing into the crowd, where they were greeted with hugs and kisses.

The DJ played another of Lena's songs and everyone was encouraged to dance, with the black lights and strobes remaining on. Jake swung Carol into his arms, pulling her into the heat and passion of the dance.

She'd never experienced anything like this before. Her heart pounded in time to the music. The lyrics of the song were sexy, the beat feverish, with Jake's big broad body bumping against hers.

This was his world. This was the kind of fast-paced party he was used to attending. She felt like a newly sprouted flower that was about to be crushed. But God help her, she liked it, too.

Because of how much she liked Jake. Everything about him thrilled her. Scared her.

Jake was singing to the song while he danced.

She shouldn't have come here. She shouldn't be swaying like the siren he'd accused her of being.

Holy island hell. Some of the couples on the dance floor were kissing, tongues and all—mimicking Lena and Mark, who were making a rowdy spectacle of themselves.

Carol's skin went hot. She hoped that Jake didn't notice the sensual activity.

Unfortunately, he did. She could tell the very moment he became aware of what was happening. He stopped singing and actually bit down on his bottom lip. Carol was doing that, too, fighting the urge to join in and press herself against Jake and kiss the living hell out of him.

Finally, the provocative song ended. The next one wasn't so bad, even if the beat was still quick and thumping.

Carol didn't know how long they danced. They didn't stop until the lights returned to normal and the ballroom settled down a bit. Guests headed for the buffet or outside to catch some air.

Jake and Carol got two frosty glasses and filled them with lemonade from the fountain. She desperately needed to quench her thirst. So did Jake apparently. He practically guzzled his.

"We should go say hello to Lena," he said.

"Yes, of course." They hadn't wished her a happy birthday yet. "Where is she?"

"I think she and Mark are over there." He motioned toward the bar.

Yep, that's where Lena and her boyfriend were. As soon as Jake and Carol approached them, Lena dived straight into Jake's arms and gave him a sisterly hug. Mark, with his fluorescent-streaked blond hair and colorfully lined eyes, grinned at Carol and said hello. Up close, she saw that he was younger than Lena, by about five years or so. Lena was blonde as well, with a long, leggy figure and doll-like features, her eyes wide and her lips bowed. She came from a showbiz family. Her parents were well-known movie stars, albeit divorced now. Even her grandmother had been a go-go dancer in the sixties, which was where the cage inspiration had probably come from.

The pop star released Jake and shifted her attention to Carol. "Do I know you?" she asked. "You seem really familiar."

"We've met briefly a few times. I'm Carol Lawrence, Jake's assistant."

"Oh, that's right. Wow. You look spectacular."

"Thank you." Carol appreciated the compliment and how genuine it sounded. "So do you. It's a wonderful party, and your entrance was magnificent."

"It was fun. A girl only turns thirty once."

Carol nodded, and after a second of silence, Lena tugged her away from the earshot of the men. But by now, the guys were already engaged in conversation, so it didn't seem to matter, anyway.

"When did you and Jake start seeing each other?" Lena asked.

Carol quickly clarified, "We're not dating."

"Yet he brought you here? On a couples-only weekend?" Lena made a curious face. "Oh, come on. Who's he trying to kid?"

"Really, it's no big deal." Carol downplayed her answer, especially with how badly she'd wanted to kiss him on the dance floor. "He needed a date for the party, and I was accessible because I work for him."

"Mark works for me, too. And now we're messing around."

Carol didn't know what to say. The comparison was making her terribly nervous. So she settled on, "Things happen."

"Do they ever." Lena leaned in close. "I am rather crazy about Mark. But who knows how long it will last? I do have a reputation for being fickle."

Carol wagged her finger, a little playfully, a little seriously. "So I've heard."

The birthday girl laughed, making no apologies. "Life is too short not to go after what you want. So whatever you do, just have a good time this weekend. You might even end up being crazy about Jake, too."

It was already too late for that. But still, Carol needed to be careful not to go overboard. She didn't live by Lena's free-spirited standards.

Their private discussion ended, and Lena went back

to her beau. Carol returned to Jake and he asked her to dance again. Only now, the music was a little slower, a little softer.

And more tempting than ever.

Four

As Jake led Carol toward the dance floor, he said, "How about if we go into one of the cages this time?" He wanted to give it a whirl.

She blinked at him. "You want to dance inside of one of those?"

"Sure. Why not? The cage Lena and Mark were in is free."

"I guess that would be okay." Carol sounded intrigued but tentative. "As long as it doesn't elevate like when they performed."

"That was just part of a show. They won't do that to us." He took her hand as they neared the cage. "But just in case, you're not afraid of heights, are you?"

"No, but you better be kidding about the 'just in case' part."

"I was." He shot her a teasing smile. He couldn't seem to get enough of her this evening.

When they reached the cage, she entered first, and he held back to study her. She looked like an exotic bird who'd just been captured, the beads on her dress winking in the light.

"What are you waiting for?" she asked.

"Nothing." He joined her inside and closed the gate.

Now that they were in there together, the space seemed tighter than he'd expected. Or maybe it just felt that way. But since the song was a ballad, it made sense for them to stand so close.

Jake took Carol in his arms, and they moved in unison, naturally compatible. They had chemistry, he thought. On and off the dance floor. In and out of the cage. She fit perfectly against him, making him want to hold her even closer.

He glanced at the big flat-screen monitor. Carol's gaze flickered to it, too. The video was a montage of movie star couples, from early Hollywood until now.

"It's funny how most of them didn't stay together," he said.

"Some of them lasted a lifetime," she replied, without missing a beat.

The lights in the ballroom went low. Even the images on the screen turned gentler, with famous wedding photos. Big frothy cakes. Long white dresses. Elegant brides and dashing grooms.

"This is beautiful," Carol said.

Was it? Jake wasn't sure. But in an oddly disturbing way, he was intrigued by the stimuli, too. It was exciting to feel what she was feeling, even if he didn't understand it.

"Maybe we shouldn't stay in here for too long," he said. The cage was starting to feel like a romantic prison, with no release in sight.

"Maybe you're right. This is getting…"

Her words drifted off, but he knew what she meant. By now, their bodies were so close they were plastered together like animals who were about to mate.

But worse yet was how the video had begun to change, morphing into film clips of love scenes, some sweet and pure, some iconic and classic, some offbeat and erotic.

"Yikes," Carol said as a bondage scene appeared.

Yeah, Jake thought. *Yikes.* It actually involved a cage. And blindfolds and all sorts of unexpected things. Trust Lena, he thought, to toss something kinky into the lovey-dovey mix.

"Let's go," he said.

Carol avoided the video, looking straight at him instead. "Where to?"

"Anywhere but here." He pushed open the gate, and they dashed out of their shiny gold confinement. They kept moving until they were outside breathing the cool night air.

But once they were in the courtyard, they both just stood there, trapped within their own private hell.

"Now what do we do?" she asked.

"I don't know." He paused to think about it. "Maybe we could go for a walk on the beach. I could really use some time away from the party."

"So could I."

He got another idea. "How about this? We can grab some food and drinks to take with us."

"That sounds nice. But how are we going to haul everything out to the beach?"

"I'll tip a waiter to pack it up for us. I'll ask him to supply a blanket or some towels or something, too." He flashed a silly grin. "Then again, maybe we can just use your dress."

She smacked his shoulder, and they both burst out laughing. It felt good to laugh. It felt good to be preparing for a picnic, too. Even if it was at night. On a tropical island.

With no one else around.

Carol walked along the beach, carrying her shoes and enjoying the sand between her toes. She looked over at Jake. His pant legs were rolled up, and he was carrying his shoes and a big square basket, filled to the brim. The waiter had even tossed in a candle from one of the tables.

"How far out are we going to go?" she asked.

"How about here?" Jake chose a spot on the other side of the estate, close enough to provide light from the mansion, but still far enough away so that the party didn't interfere.

"It's perfect." Being around so many other people, with all of that sexy activity, had been taking its toll. She was grateful for the reprieve.

Jake spread out a big fluffy beach towel and placed the basket beside it. He removed the candle, stuck it in the sand and lit the wick.

Carol sat on the towel. He joined her and handed her a champagne glass. He uncorked the Dom Pérignon and poured it.

"To peace and quiet," he said.

"The solitude is wonderful." She sipped her drink and glanced at the wax figurines. "Who was that candle fashioned after?"

"I don't know, but it smells like vanilla."

"Yes, I noticed that, too." It was a nice, pleasant aroma, mixed with the sea.

"Let's find out who they are." He lifted it up and squinted at the names across the bottom of it. "Oh, here we go. It's Robert Browning and Elizabeth Barrett Browning. I don't know much about them, do you?"

"Not really. Other than he was a playwright and they were both poets. Oh, and that they were married. I think they met through letters they exchanged."

"That's more than I knew."

"I took an English literature class in college, and I guess some of it stuck with me." Carol had a business degree from a state college that she'd funded with student loans. "It was weird, being a foster kid and trying to figure out my education. As soon as I turned eighteen, I didn't even have a place to live. But thank goodness the laws are changing now and some kids are able to stay in their foster homes until they're twenty-one."

"That's definitely a change that needed to happen. But it only involves a handful of states. Lots of foster youth are still homeless at eighteen. But I was lucky in that I was able to crash on Garrett's couch. He was back with his mom by then."

Carol nodded. Garrett wasn't orphaned like her and Jake. He'd bounced in and out of foster care because his single mother had gotten terribly ill from an infectious disease and wasn't able to care for him. At the time, she'd already been struggling with an autoimmune disorder. Although she recovered from the infection, the chronic illness continued to plague her, even now.

Jake added, "Without Garrett and his mom, I would have been totally displaced, graduating from high school with nowhere to go."

"Where was Max?"

"He was still in foster care."

"Oh, that's right. He's a little younger than you and Garrett. But you've all come a long way."

"That's for sure. Max made it first, though, being the nerd that he is."

Carol smiled, amused by Jake's description of his foster brother. Max was a self-taught software designer and internet entrepreneur who'd become a billionaire in his early twenties. But even so, she thought he was too handsome to be called a nerd. Then again, he did seem a bit socially awkward at times.

Jake said, "Max loaned Garrett and me the money

to get our businesses off the ground. We couldn't have done it without him."

"The bond between the three of you is amazing." Max's childhood had been especially troubling, from what she understood. "Where is he? I haven't seen him around lately."

"He went on a long holiday or sabbatical or whatever he's choosing to call it. I guess he needed some time alone. He can be elusive when he wants to be."

Unlike Jake, she thought, who lived his life out in the open.

"Are you cold?" he asked as a breeze kicked up. "I can give you my jacket."

She wasn't freezing by any means, but there was a bit of a chill in the air. "That would be great. Thank you."

He removed the garment and draped it around her shoulders.

Then he unpacked the food and made up a plate for her. "This looks good, doesn't it?"

"Yes, it does." She balanced the china on her lap, feeling warm and cozy with his jacket against her body.

Jake filled his plate, too, and they nibbled on an assortment of fancy appetizers and decadent desserts.

"It's a yummy combination," she said.

He met her gaze. "And we couldn't ask for a nicer setting, surrounded by the moon and the stars. You sure look pretty out here. But you've looked pretty all night."

"Even when I was a nervous wreck in the cage?"

"Yes, even then. I shouldn't have suggested that we dance in there."

"It's okay. You didn't know how it would turn out." She polished off her champagne. She had no intention of getting drunk, but a little buzz wouldn't hurt, especially with the way Jake was staring at her. She was curious to know more about him. Things she shouldn't want to know. Things she shouldn't ask. But she questioned him, anyway. "Do you do that type of stuff?"

He put his plate aside. "What stuff?"

"Like what was in the video." She refilled her glass, waiting to see what he would say. She'd heard that he was wild in bed, but no one had ever said just *how* wild. Not even the starlet who'd blogged about him had included those types of details.

"Bondage? No, I'm not into that." Without taking his eyes off her, he added, "Why...are you a secret dominatrix or something?"

If she wasn't so enraptured with him, she would have laughed. "Are you kidding? Me being a secret anything is preposterous. I just like regular sex."

"Truthfully, I was kidding. But I like it regular, too. Only, I think they call it vanilla in that lifestyle." He gestured to the vanilla-scented candle. "Like that."

Had she actually started this conversation? She put down her champagne and reached for a scone that was glazed with white icing. "This is vanilla."

Jake shifted on the towel, moving a little closer to her. "I don't think I got one of those."

"I can share it with you." She held it out to him, caught in a trap of her own making.

He took it from her, his fingertips touching hers, creating a soft stream of electricity between them.

While he bit into the pastry, she watched him, anxious to have it back, to put her mouth where his had been.

"It's good," he said.

Too good, she thought when her turn came. They continued to pass it back and forth. Carol couldn't deny that it felt like foreplay.

"What are we doing?" he asked when she finished the last bite.

"Something we shouldn't be doing," she replied. But it felt too incredible to stop.

As he leaned in to kiss her, she was thrilled, hungry for the taste of him. Their mouths came together in a burst of passion, their tongues meeting and mating.

When they stopped to catch their breaths, the candle flickered, its vanilla scent swirling around them. He took her plate off her lap, put it next to his and then moved in for the kill, nudging her down.

Again, she was too enthralled to stop him. She wanted him as close to her as possible.

He laid down on top of her, and they kissed like forbidden fiends, the sound of the ocean roaring in the distance. Carol's dress fanned out beneath her, the body veil twisting up with the towel. Jake's jacket was beneath her, too, where it had fallen off her shoulders.

He tasted like the pastry they'd shared. She probably tasted that way to him, too—sweet, sugary, filled with warmth and flavor.

She loved the weight of his body against hers, the hardness pressing down on her. Needing more, she wrapped her arms around him, trailing her hands along his spine, feeling the fabric of his shirt.

"I have fantasies about you clawing my back," he said. "I've imagined all sorts of erotic things. Even biting you." He nibbled at her ear, tugging on her lobe with his teeth. "I shouldn't want you like this, but I do."

"I shouldn't want you, either." She knew better. She was his employee. His assistant. The woman who was supposed to be so proper and composed.

His breath rushed out. "I'm so turned on right now."

"So am I." She could barely think straight.

Jake kissed her again, all rough and sexy and dark, his lips ravishing hers. Then he lifted his head and stared at her. Carol stared at him, too, her heart threatening to jump out of her skin.

Neither of them moved. If they kept going, they would end up naked in the sand, tearing each other apart.

Hot vanilla sex.

She wanted to be with him, but she couldn't let it continue, not like this. She needed to catch her breath, to clear her mind, to behave like the rational person she was.

"We need to stop," she said. Beneath her dress, her nipples were tingling, and her panties were sticking to her skin.

He sat up, his voice raspy. "I'm sorry. I didn't mean to—"

"It wasn't your fault." Carol sat forward as well, and grabbed his jacket from where it had fallen. She put it on, needing to cover up. "We both got carried away."

He frowned in the candlelight. "We should go."

She cuffed the too-long sleeves, trying to make the jacket fit her a little better. "Go where?"

"Back to our rooms. To call it a night." His frown deepened. "Unless you want to return to the party."

She cleared her plate and wrapped the uneaten food. "Goodness, no. I'd rather try to get some sleep."

"Yeah, it's probably getting late, anyway." Jake dumped out the rest of the champagne and put the empty bottle back in the basket.

Together, they cleared the evidence of their picnic, but the memory of their kisses remained, warm and wild on her lips.

He squelched the flame on the candle, pressing it between his thumb and forefinger. A moment later, he tucked the Victorian poets next to the empty bottle.

They trailed across the sand, heading for the mansion.

Once they reached the main entrance, they put on their shoes and made their way to the second floor.

As they stood in the hallway outside their rooms, she said, "We're here." It was better than saying nothing.

He set the basket on the ground, but he didn't respond.

In the silence, she attempted to smooth her mussed

hair. She could still feel the excitement of lying beneath him. Was she an idiot for having stopped it?

"My key is in my jacket," he said.

"Oh, I'm sorry." She removed the garment and handed it to him, hating to let it go. She liked being snuggled up in something that belonged to him.

"Thanks."

"You're welcome." Carol's key was in her purse. She tried for a smile. "It was quite a night."

He smiled, too. "It was, wasn't it?"

She nodded, quietly confused. "I've never really had an affair," she found herself saying. "I've only been with men I was involved with."

"You don't have to explain. I understand. That wasn't even supposed to be an issue."

"I know. But we still have two more days of hanging out together, and I don't want it to be awkward."

"I should have considered the couples-only thing a little more carefully. But I guess I just wanted to spend some time with you."

She'd had a crush on him for a long time. If she slept with him, would it get better or worse? She honestly didn't know. "I need to go." Before she did something crazy.

He waited while she unlocked her door. The key wasn't the electric card kind. It was the old-fashioned, fit-in-the-hole type. She struggled to make it work, but only because her hands were shaking.

"Do you need help?" he asked.

"No, I've got it." She finally managed. "Good night, Jake."

"Night, Carol."

She went into her room and closed the door, her pulse skittering, her emotions hanging in the balance. She flipped on the light, feeling more alone than ever.

And wishing that he was there with her.

Five

Carol didn't get ready for bed. She didn't get undressed. She didn't do anything, except battle her hunger for Jake.

Was Lena right in what she'd said? Was life too short not to go after what you wanted? Carol was beginning to think so. Or her libido certainly was.

But could she actually go through with it? And what about Jake—was he still willing? Or had he come to his senses?

She touched a finger to her lips, recalling the taste of his kisses. Should she text Jake to see how he was faring? And if she did, what should she say?

Something honest, she decided. Something to remind him that she was on the other side of those double doors.

Right. As if he was likely to forget.

She retrieved her phone and typed, Can't stop thinking about you. Then, with her heart in her throat, she hit the send button. At least she was facing her feelings.

She waited, hoping he was near his phone and hoping she'd done the right thing. She didn't have to wait long.

He answered, Me, too. About u.

Bubbling up inside, she felt like a teenager conversing with her longtime crush. She hastily wrote, Don't know what to do about it.

He replied, Are u in bed?

No. Still in my clothes.

So am I. Except my shirt.

Carol imagined how he looked, bare-chested and tousled from the beach, tapping out intimate little things to her.

This is weird, she texted him.

I know. Really weird. But I like it.

Me, too. Sort of seems like we're sexting.

Yeah, it does. A second later, he asked, If I invited u to my room, would u come over?

Her pulse jumped. But just to be sure that he meant what he said, she inquired, Do you want me to come over for real? Or are we only fantasizing about it?

He popped off a quick, Yes, I want u to come over. For real.

She released the breath in her lungs and replied, Give me a few minutes.

To think about it?

To come over. She didn't want to keep thinking about it. She just wanted to be with him.

He wrote, Excited to see u.

She was excited, too. And she wanted to look refreshed, to comb her hair and reapply her lipstick.

Before this went any further, she asked, Do you have what we'll need? They couldn't do this without protection.

Yes, he told her. It's not a problem.

Then I'll be there soon, she wrote.

I'll be waiting, he replied.

Unlock the door on your side, she reminded him.

I will came his reply.

If Carol was the brazen sort, she would untie the front of her dress, take a seductive selfie and send it to him. But she wasn't that kind of girl. Already, she was stepping outside of her comfort zone. But she wasn't going to back out. She was going through with this, no matter how nervous she was.

She went into the bathroom to freshen up, warning

herself to relax. Not that it would change anything. Calm or nervous. Shy or bold. She was going to make love with her boss.

And she needed to be with Jake tonight. She needed to finish what they'd started at the beach, to feel his aroused body next to hers, to kiss him with unbridled lust, to rake her nails down his back.

Once she looked presentable, Carol walked over to the doors that divided them. A few breathless beats later, she crossed the threshold.

Jake was waiting for her, just as he said he would be. He looked tall and dark and stunning: wearing no shirt, no shoes, just his trousers. By now, she was barefoot, too.

Their gazes met, and he smiled, as if he was about to commit a secret little crime.

But he was, wasn't he?

Mesmerized, she moved closer. There were so many facets to that smile, so many ways in which it defined him.

"What kind of trouble did you get into?" she asked, reaching out to skim his jaw, her fingers igniting from the feeling.

He leaned into her touch. "What are you talking about?"

"When you were young," she explained.

He shrugged, lifting his shoulders, as if he were knocking the weight of her curiosity off them. "The usual."

To her, there was nothing usual about getting into

trouble. She'd done everything in her power to toe the line, to be the kind of kid who didn't make waves. "Did you ever do anything really bad?"

"What do you mean? Like break the law?"

She nodded and waited for him to reply. She couldn't begin to guess if he had a juvenile record. At the moment, all she knew was how dangerous he still seemed, all grown-up.

"Yes," he said. "I got caught once."

"Doing what?"

"It isn't important now."

"It is to me." To understand the boy he once was, to make love with the sexually charged man he'd become.

He took her in his arms. "We can talk about it later."

He was right. This wasn't the time to discuss it. She closed her eyes, losing herself in the sweet flutter of letting him hold her.

Then Jake ruggedly whispered, "I want to strip you. Tell me I can. Tell me to do it."

With a jolt of excitement, she opened her eyes and looked into his. "Yes, do it. As fast as you want."

He didn't hurry, even if she'd just given him permission. Ever so gently, he removed the body veil that was draped around her dress. The fabric fell away, drifting to the floor. He continued his quest, untying the sarong. As he unwrapped the dress, she struggled to steady herself.

"It's okay," he said. "You won't fall. I've got you."

She was already falling, tumbling into a highly forbidden zone. He tossed her sarong over a chair, and

Carol did her darnedest not to feel self-conscious, even if she was wearing nothing but a pair of beige silk panties.

Jake took her hand and led her straight to his bed. Her skin pulsed as she prepared for what came next.

As she lay there, amid his rumpled sheets, he said, "You're incredible."

So was he. Too incredible for words. She could barely believe that she was in his company, with him climbing on top of her.

He zeroed in on her nipples, teasing each one, going back and forth, moving his tongue in sexy little swirls. She thought she might die from the thrill of it.

He lifted his head and smiled. "Should I do it some more?"

Put his mouth on her breasts? "Yes, please."

"You're so polite. Such a good girl."

She didn't deny his claim, and this time, when he resumed the activity, she tunneled her fingers through his hair.

She sighed as he ran his hand along the waistband of her panties, teasing her, making her limbs quaver.

The lights were on, shining as bright as the sun. Only, it was dark outside, with stars dancing in the night.

He peeled her panties all the way off, and now she was naked, except for the earrings and bracelet he'd given her.

"What about these?" she asked about the jewels. "Should they come off, too?"

"No. I like how you look in them."

"I'm trying not to worry."

"About what? Keeping the jewelry? It's just a few little baubles."

"I was talking about how we're going to feel in the morning." She didn't want to regret what they were doing. But she feared there would be repercussions.

"Tomorrow doesn't matter. All that matters is tonight."

He gestured to the condoms he'd scattered on the nightstand. "I didn't pack these purposely. But am I ever glad that they were in my luggage."

She put her hands against his chest, where she could feel the strong steady beats of his heart. "They just happened to be there?"

He nodded. "From the last time I traveled. I even thought about it when we were on the plane. But I didn't think I'd be using them."

She trailed her fingers down his body. No doubt about it, there was going to be hell to pay later on. Anything this exciting would have consequences.

Once she reached his stomach, she followed the ripple of muscle along his abs. She was familiar with his workout routine and how disciplined he was about it. He'd built an employee gym at the office for everyone to use, himself included. He had a weight room at home, too. His main residence was a glittering estate in the Hollywood Hills, with a tennis court and a poolside view of the city. Carol had been there a number of times, either running errands for him or dropping off urgent documents for him to sign. And now she was exploring his half-naked body, with a different kind of urgency coiling inside her.

He unzipped his pants, but he didn't remove them. Nonetheless, she noticed that he wasn't wearing underwear. But she wasn't surprised. He seemed like a commando guy.

He said, "There are so many things I want to do to you."

Delicious things, she thought. He put his fingers between her legs, rubbing that one little spot, making her moan from the pleasure. Everything was warm and sexy, including the sheets beneath her skin. She moaned again, trying to contain herself.

He shifted his weight, his big, broad body casting a shadow over hers. Then he took the foreplay a step further, going down on her with his mouth.

She couldn't stop touching him while he did it: the breadth of his shoulders, the messiness of his hair, the handsome angles of his face. She even touched herself, where his tongue made contact. There were no bounds, no limits, just heat and primal hunger, shooting straight to her core, making her unbearably wet.

As the orgasm built, her nerve endings electrified. She was steeped in so many sensations, so many hungers, all at once.

Jake didn't stop until the last spasm racked her body, dragging her under his spell.

He kissed her afterward, barely giving her time to recover. But she didn't care. He took off his pants, and she saw that he was desperately aroused. She lowered her hand, closing it around him.

While she stroked him, he kissed her once again, heightening the passion. She tightened her grip, wanting to make him feel extra good. But all too soon, he reached for a condom. He was leaking at the tip.

When he extended the packet to her, she widened her eyes. "Why are you…?"

"Because I want to watch you put it on me."

"No one has ever asked me to do that before. Whenever I've been with someone, the guy always…"

"You know how, don't you?"

"Yes, of course. But you'd be better at it, I'm sure. Quicker. More efficient."

"It's not a contest, Carol." He smiled naughtily. "It's just a little fun between lovers."

She opened the packet, feeling as if she was all thumbs. But it was only because she was so darned anxious to be with him. By the time she managed to put the condom in place, he was harder than hard and sexier than hell.

And just like that, he nudged her legs apart and thrust into her, stealing what was left of her breath and making her want him even more.

Jake marveled at this moment, taking a second to process it. He was inside of Carol. His marriage-minded assistant. How crazy was that?

He thrust deeper, and she gasped, closing around

him in hot, slick pleasure. This was sex at its most fundamental level, boiled down to raw need.

Need. The word punched him like a fist. Jake didn't know what was wrong with him, not having been able to control his hunger for her. She was right about tomorrow. They would have to figure things out. Normally he didn't concern himself with incidentals. But he was in bed with a woman who worked for him. That wasn't something that could be ignored.

But for now, morning was a ways away.

Taking what he wanted, what he craved, he kissed his newfound lover with heat and vigor. Twin moans escaped their lips. She wrapped her legs around him, and he moved his mouth to her neck and bared his teeth, nipping her skin.

Euphoria surged through him, so right, so wrong, so hot and pulsing. Was this how addicts felt when they slammed drugs into their veins?

Jake rolled over so Carol could straddle him. While she rode him, he touched her, cupping her breasts and thumbing her nipples. He liked how pink and pretty and pebbled they were.

She braced her hands on his shoulders, digging her nails into his flesh.

"Harder," he said.

With those neat lady's nails still sharply in place, she rode him deeper, doubling the euphoria. As she rocked forward, setting an erotic pace, a breeze from the window stirred the ghostly white curtains, sweeping air through the room.

Jake imagined that the sea was rising, crashing in orgasmic waves, coming closer and closer to the moon-lit shore.

Caribbean fever, he thought. He had it bad.

"I promised myself that I wasn't going to seduce you this weekend," he said. "And now I am."

Her hair fell forward, soft and shiny around her face. "Yes, you definitely are. But I had a hand in it, too."

"Yeah, you did." She had sent him that text urging him to be with her. He switched positions again, gulping frantic breaths in between numerous kisses.

Once he was on top, he pounded her harder and faster. By now, she was clawing his back.

Was she leaving long, sexy scratch marks? Telltale signs of passion? He hoped so. He wanted to be marred by her, to have every aspect of his fantasy fulfilled.

His skin was filled with fire, tattoos and all. Uncta was going into shape-shifting mode, and Eskeilay was hopping through the grass in her earth-womb.

"Don't stop," she said.

As if he could. He was on autopilot, moving like a sex machine, desperate to come.

So was Carol apparently. She met him stroke for stroke, maneuvering her body in ways that maximized the pleasure. Only, she seemed to be doing it naturally, unaware that she was so sexy. Jake actually envied the Goody Two-shoes who married her, simply because the lucky stiff would get to be with her every night.

"You're a hellcat in bed," he said.

Her voice went husky. "I'm not, not usually…"

"So I just bring it out in you?"

"I don't know." She clawed the crap out of him again. "Probably."

He gazed into her glowing green eyes. Was this how she would behave on her wedding night? Sweet and sensual and animalistic? "Your future husband can thank me later."

She writhed beneath him. "You're cocky, Jake."

He glanced down at where their bodies were joined. "So I am."

She followed his line of sight. "That isn't what I meant."

"Then why are you enjoying the view?"

"For the same reason you are."

Because being together was exciting. Because they both wanted to remember how it felt. How it looked.

Jake shifted his hips, making the moment hotter.

In. Out. Deep. Deeper.

Carol gasped, and a haze of hunger enveloped him, his body jerking, his erection pulsing, his vision glazing till he could barely see at all. She was falling, too, his orgasm triggering hers. Or maybe hers had jump-started his? He was too far gone to know.

Sensations slammed between them, and she clung to him, making breathy sounds in his ear. His personal assistant.

His *very* personal assistant, he amended.

When it was over Jake was beaded with sweat. He withdrew and dropped down on top of Carol, needing to drag as much air into his lungs as he could get. But what he got was the scent of sex, mingled with her citrus perfume.

She skimmed her fingers down his spine. Gone were her claws. There was just softness now.

"Am I hurting you?" he asked.

She nuzzled his shoulder. "Isn't it a little late to be asking me that?"

He grinned in spite of himself. "I meant, am I too heavy?"

"No, you're good." She traced his tailbone. "I'm not an itty-bitty breakable thing. I can take it."

He could have stayed there all night, luxuriating in her curves, except that he needed to get rid of the condom. "I'll be right back."

Jake got up and went into the bathroom to do his thing. When he returned, she was sitting forward in bed, with the sheet partially covering her.

"I should take a picture of you," he said. Beside her, the ghostly curtains were billowing again.

She tugged the sheet closer. "You better not."

It was tempting, to say the least. "You just look so pretty, that's all." Mussed up and wearing the jewelry he'd given her.

"Thank you, but we don't need that kind of evidence from this night." She patted the space next to her. "Now, come back to bed."

"Yes, ma'am." He hopped into the spot she offered. "So what kind do we need?"

"What kind of what?"

"Evidence from this night?"

She butted her shoulder against his. "Smart aleck."

He shrugged, smiled, got closer to her. For the heck of it, he gave her a noisy kiss, and they slid down onto the pillows together.

"I'm not much of a cuddler," he said.

"Then you're doing a good job, considering."

He was trying. "You seem like the type who would like it."

She sighed. "I am. I do."

I do. He frowned at her choice of words, feeling the weight of them. Someday, she was going to find a nice, proper guy. Someday, she would become someone's honeymoon bride.

But for now she was in bed with Jake, snuggling against him, all warm and cozy, where they both knew she didn't belong.

Six

Carol awakened early. The room was bathed in soft morning hues. She noticed that the window was still open, but there was less of a breeze.

She'd slept soundly beside her lover. Too soundly, she decided. And now she was anything but calm.

She glanced over at Jake. Sometime during the night, he must have shifted onto his side because they weren't facing each other anymore. His back was turned and he was sprawled out, one leg inside the covers, the other one exposed, along with a portion of his naked butt.

Heaven almighty. What had she done?

A foolish question, if there ever was one. She knew darn well what she'd done. She'd gone into this with her eyes wide open.

She sat up and steadied her breath. She needed coffee, but first she was going to wash the remnants of makeup off her face, tame her hair and brush her teeth. Rather than trudge off to her bathroom without any clothes, she located her sarong and wrapped it around herself.

Just as she was preparing to slip away, Jake rolled over, nearly giving her a heart attack. She'd assumed he was dead asleep.

"Hey," he said with a graveled voice and a half smile.

"Hi." Did he have to look so good, so handsome and wild, with a bit of overnight beard stubble? "I'm going to freshen up, then make coffee. Want some?"

"Sure." He sat forward, dragged a hand through his hair and squinted into the hazy patch of sunlight that spilled over him. "I need to hit the head, too."

"Okay. I'll see you in a few."

As he climbed out of bed, Carol darted off and practically stumbled over her body veil. She picked it up, but she didn't take the time to look for her panties. Uncertain of what Jake had done with them after he'd peeled them off her, she would search for them later.

She continued to her room, and once she was standing at her bathroom mirror, she removed her bracelet. She'd actually slept in it. The earrings, too, so she took those off, as well.

Then, after she was fresh and somewhat tidy, with her sarong tied a little tighter, she prepared the coffee in the single-serve machine in her room, making each cup separately. She added sugar to Jake's, the way he liked it. This wasn't the first time she'd sweetened his coffee and it probably wouldn't be the last. But it felt different from before.

Everything did.

Because she'd had sex with her boss. Wild, delicious, sheet-tumbling, tongue-kissing, body-scorching sex.

She brought the coffee to his room, trying to keep her hands from shaking. Jake was back in bed, looking as if he'd splashed a bit of water on his face, too. He certainly seemed more awake. She handed him his cup, and he thanked her.

Instead of joining him in bed, Carol opted for a nearby chair. He was still naked, except that he had a pillow on his lap, to protect himself from the hot beverage, she assumed.

Struggling to stay focused, she sipped her coffee, a perfect brew for a nervous day—strong and rich and aromatic.

"Are you concerned about last night?" he asked.

Lying would get her nowhere. Besides, her emotions were probably written all over her face. "It definitely feels weird now that it's over."

"Yeah, it does. But we knew what we were getting into when we did it."

"That's for sure." They couldn't behave as if they weren't aware of their actions. "Morning was bound to come."

Falling silent, he let his gaze roam over her, his eyes dark and intense. Then he said, "I don't think it should end like this."

She blinked, not quite catching his drift. "What?"

"Us. The sex. We should keep doing it all weekend."

Confused, Carol debated what to say. She glanced at the nightstand, where the rest of the condoms were. "You want to do it some more, even though you agreed that it seems weird?"

"Ending it so quickly will make it even weirder. We might as well make the most of this couples-only thing. And there's no denying how hot we are together."

No, there was no denying it. She could still feel the forbidden thrill of their union. The warm, slick foreplay. The hard-driving rhythm. The orgasmic shivers.

Every moment was embedded in her brain. In her body. Even in parts of her soul. It had been the most exciting night of her life. But the most irresponsible, too.

Dare she repeat it over the next few days? "Are you sure we shouldn't just cut our losses now?"

"And do what for the rest of the time that we're here? Hang out at the beach and pretend it didn't happen? Better to embrace it, I think."

Her pulse jumped. "By getting naked again?"

"I'm already bare. And under that pretty dress of yours, so are you." He set his coffee aside. "Aren't you?"

"Yes." Her voice all but quavered. She hadn't put any underwear on this morning. She still had no idea where her panties from last night were, either. Maybe stuck in the bedcovers somewhere?

"So what's it going hurt?" he asked. "A weekend of fun, sun and great sex. Things could be worse."

"What about the other guests here? Are we going to try to hide it from them?"

"I don't see why we should. Besides, most of them probably already assumed that we were a couple, anyway."

She thought about her conversation with Lena and how it had influenced her to sleep with Jake to begin with. "Lena predicted it."

"She did?"

"When we talked at the party. But we can't let anyone figure it out when we get home. I can't handle people at work knowing."

"I agree. It'll be over as soon as we leave the island. We won't ever do it again, and no one at the office will be the wiser. It'll be our secret. But for now, I think we should enjoy each other's company." He held out his hand, beckoning her. "Come on, Carol. Indulge me."

Sweet mercy, she thought. He was just too charming to resist. As she left her chair and came forward, he pulled her into his arms and kissed the living daylights out of her.

She rolled over the bed with him, letting him untie her sarong. He put his hands all over her naked body. She did the same thing to him, exploring that gorgeous golden-brown skin and those strong, sculpted muscles. She couldn't stop touching him.

They'd both staked their claims, and now it was official. They were having a fling. A weekend rendezvous. A mind-spinning affair.

"Take a shower with me," he said. "I want to get wet with you."

She circled her arms around him, pressing her body closer to his. "You're already making me wet."

He lowered his hand, spreading her, testing her, teasing her. "That goes with the territory."

She moaned from the pressure building between her thighs. "A shower sounds amazing."

"Then let's go." He withdrew his fingers. "We can finish this in there."

Carol wanted him to finish her, as many times as he could. They sat up, and he removed a condom from the nightstand.

She took stock of the inventory. "Do you have any more of those in your luggage?"

He fisted the packet. "No, just these."

"There will only be three left after we use that one."

He smiled, then jerked his head, his hair falling across his forehead. "That's not enough for two more days?"

She smiled, too, anxious to climb into the shower with him. "I don't know. Is it?"

"I guess we're going to have to pace ourselves."

So far, they weren't doing a particularly good job of that. It wasn't even noon yet, and already they were gearing up for water-drenched sex.

They entered his bathroom, where the contents from his shaving kit were strewn about the counter. He'd left his toothbrush and toothpaste out, too, with the tube uncapped. Carol never did that.

Of course Jake had a housekeeper who came to his house at least once a week. He had a chef who put healthy meals in his fridge, too. He'd become accustomed to people looking after his needs.

But not always, Carol reflected. He was an orphaned child, just like her, a kid who knew what it was like to be alone, with barely anyone to care.

He turned on the shower, and as soon as it was warm enough, they stepped into the clear glass enclosure. The luxuriously designed stall was big enough for two, fitting them comfortably.

They took turns under the spray, and he helped her shampoo her hair. She'd never had a man do that for her before, and it felt wonderful. He soaped down her body, too.

Slow and sudsy.

Carol washed him as well, working her way down, until she was on her knees, rinsing him clean.

"Damn," he said, tangling his fingers through her wet hair.

She took him in her mouth. He was big and hard and getting harder with every stroke. She wasn't normally this bold, but she wasn't going to waste a second of their time together.

He moved with her, watching her, keeping his hands in her hair. But he didn't let her bring him to completion.

"My turn," he told her, changing places with her.

When Jake dropped to his knees, Carol shivered from head to toe. He was determined to make her come, and she was more than happy to let him do whatever he wanted.

Her boss had become her undoing, her vice, her craving, her full-blown, take-me, have-me, I'm-yours hunger. She didn't want to think about how difficult it was going to be when they went home, when it was over for good, so she tried to block that from her mind.

He used his hands and his mouth. He satisfied every yearning she had, being the beautifully skilled lover that he was.

The climax he gave her rocked her to the core. She shook and shuddered and gulped the steam that was rising.

Jake stood up and tore into the condom wrapper. He put on the protection hastily and slammed into her.

Carol was going to relive this encounter for the rest of her supposedly proper life. It would never fade into oblivion, not even in a million years. She memorized everything: the hammering motion, the pounding spray from the showerhead, the bar of soap that had fallen and was spinning around the drain.

"I've got you where I want you," he said, rasping the words, breathing heavily.

"I've got you, too." She raked her nails over every part of him she could reach, and he rewarded her with a rough groan, proving how much he liked it.

They kissed in wild desperation. They even clanked their teeth, making frantic love, their hips thrusting to a powerful rhythm.

Then he said, "I'm not usually a morning person."

She smiled, laughed, gazed at him through the thickness of the steam. "You could have fooled me."

He laughed, too, looking wild and boyish, yet warm and protective. He held her tighter, and she stopped clawing him, using her fingertips to soothe the places she'd scratched.

They kissed again, only not quite so brutally this time.

Somewhere in the middle of the mania was friendship. The knowledge, she supposed, that they shared a childhood bond. That they'd lost everything, and now they had one crazy weekend, wrapped up together in bouts of guilty pleasure.

His release was strong and convulsive, and Carol absorbed the friction when he came, taking everything he was, everything about him, into her body. Until there was nothing left but the sound of running water.

After the shower, Carol and Jake ordered breakfast and had it delivered to Jake's room. Carol was grateful that Lena had hired a staff that could be trusted, who wouldn't sell tidbits to the tabloids or take unauthorized pictures.

Of course, Jake wasn't a big-time celebrity. His "Beefcake Bachelor" status wasn't enough to make him a star. No one followed him around, the way they did Lena and some of her other guests. But thank goodness this weekend was private, either way.

"Do you want to eat outside?" he asked.

"Sure. Why not?" Carol thought it sounded nice and relaxing.

He carried the tray onto the veranda, and they sat across from each other at a glass-topped table. She gazed out at the view. The pool area was vacant, almost eerily quiet.

"I wonder if anyone else is even up yet," he said.

"Some of them are probably hungover from the party." She cut into her eggs. She'd chosen poached, topped with cheese, tomatoes and pesto. "And the rest of them might just be lazing around like we are."

"Yeah." He was eating a sausage and egg scramble. "We haven't even gotten dressed yet."

She nodded. Both of them were in their robes, and her towel-dried hair was still slightly damp. She'd combed it straight down, though. He'd only run his fingers through his, barely taming his thick dark locks. But his unkempt look was a part of who he was.

"So," she said, still curious to know about his youthful rebellions, "what did you get caught doing when you were young?"

He made a face. "I stole things. Mostly video games and DVDs and stuff like that. Sometimes I would nab a bottle of booze, just for the hell of it." He frowned at his food. "But my biggest thrill was lifting trinkets for the girls I liked. I'd have them show me what they wanted, then I'd go back on my own to steal it. That's what I got popped for. Taking this little diamond necklace from a department store."

She studied him in the balcony light, the way the shade played over his face. "The store pressed charges?"

"Yep. I was arrested for shoplifting."

"And now you buy women pricey gifts to make amends for what you did?"

He glanced up from his plate. "I never really thought about it that way, but I suppose I do." He paused, fork in hand. "Or maybe it just makes me feel good, being able to afford to give them pretty things."

Like the jewelry he'd given her, she thought.

"I started stealing about six months after my family died," he said. "I was so freaked out in foster care I could barely stand it. I needed something that made me feel alive. That gave me a sense of purpose, even if I knew it was wrong. I was fifteen when I got busted, so it had been going on for a while before I got caught."

Carol questioned him further, piecing his past together in her mind. "Did Garrett and Max know what you were doing?"

"Yes, but they didn't say anything to me about it. They had enough problems of their own."

"What happened after you got arrested?"

"I was put on probation. But I stopped stealing. Not because I got busted, but because my caseworker said that if I didn't get my act together, I would be moved to a group home, where the setting would be much more restrictive. And I didn't want to go someplace where I would be separated from Garrett and Max."

She sipped her orange juice. "So in a sense, they saved you? Just by being there?"

"They definitely did. We had our heritage in common, too, which also helped us stay together. We were placed in Native American foster homes, and there weren't all that many, compared to nonnative ones. The only way we were likely to be separated or never see each other again was if I screwed up and went to a group home." Jake had a thoughtful expression. "Soon after that, Max came up with the idea for us to band together. To work toward becoming megarich someday."

Carol considered the situation. "Max came from a really poor environment, didn't he?"

"Poor. Abusive. The works. He had all kinds of motivation to want to be rich and respected. So did Garrett, with how badly he wanted to keep a roof over his mother's head and keep her well. But me…? There was nothing I wanted, except my family back. But then I figured there was nothing wrong with having fancy houses and fast cars." He looked directly across the table at her, flirtation alive in his eyes. "And beautiful women, of course."

Heat unfurled in her loins. "Yes, of course."

"Sex was always an outlet for me. I was fifteen the first time it happened."

"The same year you got caught shoplifting?"

He nodded. "I was already sleeping with the girl I nabbed the necklace for. She was my first. What a rush that was, having a girl want me like that."

Carol wasn't surprised that he was having sex at such a young age. She had waited until college, with her first serious boyfriend. "And you've had lots of lovers since."

"Being rich helps."

"Your money doesn't matter to me," she told him. "That's not why I'm here with you."

"I know. But mostly women want to date me because I'm rich, even the ones who are trying to heal me. But you won't try to do that because you're already broken, too."

She didn't know whether to be offended by his assessment of her or impressed that he knew enough to call himself broken. To combat her uncertainty, she said, "You and I aren't going to be together long enough for me to try to do anything, except get through this weekend without those condoms running out."

He grinned and topped off his orange juice. "Touché, Miss Lawrence." When she furrowed her brow, he stopped smiling, the abrupt change hardening his handsome features. "Come on, Carol. Don't be upset because I said you were messed up, too."

"Did I say I was upset?"

"No, but I can tell it bothered you."

She gazed out at the pool. It was still vacant, the water rippling on its own, the chaise longues and chairs empty. Suddenly the entire island seemed lonely, even the parts she couldn't see. "Your opinion of me is confusing."

"Why? Because you think that you're handling being orphaned better than I am? No one gets by unscathed. No one," he reiterated softy. "Not even you."

Seven

Later that day, Carol and Jake gathered on the beach with Lena and Mark and a slew of other couples. Lena had suggested that everyone pitch in to build a sand-castle, which had morphed into a whimsical fortress, surrounded by sculptures of dragons and dolphins and mermaids. So far, the results were spectacular, but this was a creative crowd. Some of the attendees were set designers and special effects artists, and they were spearheading the project, offering help where it was needed.

Jake and Carol were on one of the mermaid teams, sitting off by themselves, shaping the sand. Their mermaid wasn't half-bad. In fact, she was rather pretty, with her curvy figure and flowing hair.

Jake glanced up at Carol, but she averted her gaze. He was molding the mermaid's breasts, and she was working on the tail, giving it texture. She was also thinking about what he'd said about her being broken. No matter how hard she tried, she just couldn't seem to forget his unsettling opinion of her.

"What's wrong?" he asked.

"Nothing," she replied.

"You seem preoccupied."

"I'm just trying to focus on this."

"Are you sure that's all it is?"

She decided to come clean. Otherwise, it would keep affecting her mood. "Do you really think I'm messed up?"

He stopped molding the mermaid and sat back on his haunches. "I didn't mean it in an offensive way, Carol."

"Then how did you mean it?"

"I was just saying how losing your family was as traumatic for you as it was for me." He squinted at her, the sun shining in his eyes. "It's unfortunate, too, that neither of us had any extended family who could take us in. Or I assume that you didn't or you wouldn't have been placed in the system."

"You're right. There was no one. Both of my parents were raised by single moms, and they were gone by then. Well, actually, my dad's mom was still around, but she had cancer and was too sick to step in and help. She died about a year later." Carol sighed, pushing away the tightness in her chest. "I also had an uncle on my dad's side, but he was a young man in the military, so he couldn't raise me. He used to write me letters after my parents died, keeping a connection going, but then he was killed in Iraq." Another death that had destroyed her all over again. "But I managed to get through it, just as I got through losing everyone else."

"How? By being overly good and proper? How is that any better than me running wild?"

Irked by the comparison, she defended herself. "I'm not being overly good and proper now. I'm here with you, on this island, sharing your damned bed."

"My *damned* bed, huh?" he mimicked her, a slow and sexy smile spreading across his face. "Is this our first fight?"

She rolled her eyes. She even smiled a little. It was silly to make a fuss over it. But that didn't stop her from being caught up in the past. It didn't stop Jake, either, apparently.

He said, "I had Garrett and Max to help me through it. I had Garrett's mom, too. But who did you have, Carol, especially after your uncle was gone?"

She kept her response light, determined to stay strong, rather than dredge up all of that old pain. "Some of my foster parents were really nice people. Of course, some were indifferent, too. So mostly I just learned to do it on my own, to not rely too heavily on anyone else."

He wiped his hands on his swim trunks. "Yes, but how?"

"By doing everything that I thought was right. By studying in school and getting good grades. By being respectful to my elders. By being as responsible as I could." She stared straight at him. "I wanted to do the kinds of things that would make my parents proud. I wanted them to be looking down on me from heaven, saying, 'Look how far she's come.'"

"That's nice. Really, truly it is. But it sounds lonely, too. Didn't you ever want to rebel? To scream and rage?"

"No. Staying calm kept me sane."

"That would have made me crazy."

There were plenty of times that she'd cried herself to sleep. But she'd refused to take her grief out on the world, the way he had. "What's the deal with your extended family? Why wasn't there anyone who could raise you?"

He returned to the mermaid, absently running his fingers over the areas he'd already shaped. "My dad was an only child, and his parents died before I was born, so that ruled them out." He spoke slowly, as if he were plucking the memories from his mind. "My maternal grandfather was still around, though, and so was my mom's sister. Grandpa lived in Ohio, where my mom was originally from, and my aunt was in Arizona, where she'd relocated years before. But at the time of the accident, she was going through a divorce, and the last thing she needed was another kid. She already had two little boys of her own and was struggling to raise them. One of them was a baby, three, maybe four months old, and the other one was a toddler, just barely out of diapers."

"What about your grandfather?"

"He said that he couldn't afford to accommodate me. Granted, he was just a working-class guy, but it was more than a money issue. He just didn't want to get saddled with one of his grandkids. He'd already raised his daughters by himself."

"When your grandmother died?" she asked, curious about the rest of the story.

A muscle ticked in Jake's jaw. "She didn't die. She left him for another man, abandoning him and their daughters when the girls were still pretty young. It tore everyone apart. Grandpa resented being left with the kids, and my mom and my aunt bore the brunt of his anger. They suffered from their mother leaving, too, of course. They were crushed by what she'd done."

"That's awful." Carol couldn't fathom a woman walking out on her children.

"Needless to say, they weren't a tight-knit family. Even when my mom was still alive, Grandpa rarely came to see to us. We hardly ever visited him, either. He remained distant with my aunt and her kids, too. He didn't help them when they needed it."

"Where is he now?"

"He has Alzheimer's, so he doesn't remember any of this, anyway. He's in a treatment center that looks after him. He's too far gone to be on his own."

"Who pays for that?"

"I do."

She figured as much. Jake didn't seem like the type of person to turn his back on someone, even if they'd turned their back on him. "So your mom and your aunt weren't close, either?"

"No. But my mom made up for her upbringing with how loving she was with us. With me and my dad and my sisters," he clarified.

Carol knew what he meant. "How did your aunt react when your mom died?"

"She was devastated, and guilty, I think, because they hadn't kept in better touch. She apologized at the time for not being able to take me in. But I understood how bad things were for her. She could barely feed her own children."

"How is she now?"

"She's doing fine. I encouraged her to get a real estate license, and now she works for an associate of mine who flips houses in Arizona. I'm putting my cousins through college, too, so they'll have a chance for a promising future, without being burdened by student loans."

Carol was still paying on her loans, but she had a good job and a generous boss who provided a discount on her rent. Without Jake, she wouldn't be making it as easily as she was. "That's nice of you."

"Thanks. My aunt appreciates everything I've done for her and her kids. But we haven't bonded, not in a way that feels like blood." He shrugged it off. "Maybe someday we will. But what matters most to me is my foster brothers. They're my true family."

Carol nodded. After hearing the whole story, she understood more about his loyalty to them.

"I still can't relate to how you handled being orphaned," he said, bringing the discussion back to her.

She took a moment to think about her response, to delve deeper into her history. "Being responsible is in my nature." She couldn't change that about herself, nor did she want to. "But being creative helped, too. I felt better when I learned to quilt. One of my foster mothers and her neighbors used to make quilts, and they showed me how to do it, too. The first one I worked on with them was a scrap quilt, made from fabrics they traded with one another. Some quilters collect scraps like trading cards." She paused, then added, "But the main reason quilting became so therapeutic for me is when I started making them by myself I would choose fabrics that reminded me of my family. It was like piecing together my memories and keeping them alive."

Jake watched her work on the mermaid, almost as if he were imagining watching her sew. "Did you make a quilt that represented your hopes and dreams, too? Did you put fabrics together that embodied your future husband and the kids you were going to have?"

Stunned by how spot-on he was, Carol met his gaze. He was keeping a close eye on her. So close it made her feel like a ladybug under a microscope. "What makes you think I did that?"

"It just seems like something you would've done, with how you used to fantasize about your wedding."

"You're right. I did make a quilt like that." She wasn't going to pretend otherwise. "I used a fancy white fabric to symbolize my dress. To showcase my kids, I used baby prints—pink teddy bears for a girl and blue dinosaurs for a boy."

"What about for your husband? What did you use to represent him?"

"A shiny black tuxedo material." She'd never really pictured what her groom would look like, other than that he would be dressed in formal wear. "I used a red rose pattern, too, because those are the flowers I envisioned in the ceremony."

"Do you still have it?"

"Yes. I saved all of my old quilts." She had them tucked away in her room. They were an important part of her childhood, of her heart, of the person she'd become. "Do you still think I'm broken?"

"Yes, but in a really sweet way." He sent her a teasing smile, even if he was still watching her just as closely as before.

"Okay, Mr. Juvenile Delinquent." She reached into the sand, dug around and found a shell, intending to throw it at him. But she held on to it instead, thinking how pretty it was. "You and your stolen jewelry."

"Thank goodness I got caught, huh? Or I might have become a cat burglar instead of the privileged playboy that I am today."

Privileged indeed. He'd carved out quite a life for himself. "Someday my dreams are going to come true, too."

His expression changed, his smile fading, his tone much more serious. "For a big white wedding?"

She glanced at the shell. She was still holding it, the

chevron shape fitting delicately into her hand. "I want a family. I always have."

"Just be happy, no matter what you do."

"I will." She placed the shell in the mermaid's hair, using it as decoration.

"That looks nice," Jake said. "Should we collect more of those?"

Carol nodded, and they both sifted through the sand, together yet somehow still alone.

At dusk the guests had dinner on the beach, prepared by the chef and his team. Although vegetable skewers and salads were available, the main dish was a seafood boil, lightly seasoned and served with a traditional tartar sauce or a spicy salsa, if you preferred your food with a bit of a kick.

Tons of fires had been built, either for large groups of people who wanted to socialize or for couples who preferred to be by themselves, which was what Jake and Carol had chosen.

While they ate, they sat on a big fluffy blanket at their own cozy little fire. He couldn't think of a nicer way to spend the evening, especially with how mesmerized Carol seemed.

"Look how enchanted everything is," she said, gazing out into the distance.

He followed her line of sight. The completed sand-castle had been decorated with hundreds of candles, creating an otherworldly effect. The majestic architecture presented soaring pillars, domed archways and flying buttresses. The detail was magnificent, even from across the beach.

She spoke softly, reverently. "I can see our mermaid from here."

"I see her, too." Their sculpture was surrounded by twinkling lights.

"I feel so protective of her. The way she's beckoning the sea with her beauty."

Jake turned to look at Carol, impressed with how beautiful she was, too. She wore a shiny mesh cover-up over her bikini, and her hair was pinned loosely on top of her head, a few silky strands falling about her face. "Don't worry. She can handle her own."

"Not when the tide comes in. Everything will be gone then."

"That's part of the magic. Nothing is supposed to last forever."

"Like this weekend?" she asked with a faraway sound in her voice.

"Yes, like this trip." As he admired Carol's profile, he realized that he'd neglected to share an important part of his past with her. "You're never going to believe what I forgot to tell you."

"What?" she asked, finally turning toward him.

"The Choctaw mermaid legend." Of all things to forget, he thought, after they'd spent half the day making one.

She shifted on the blanket, like an eager child settling in for a ghost story, her food half-eaten. "You can tell me now."

Jake collected his thoughts, recalling the story as it had been told to him. "They're called 'white people of the water' because they have pale, trout-like skin. They live in the bayou, in the deepest part of the water. But where it's clear, too. They aren't murky creatures."

Firelight shone in her eyes. "Are they beautiful, like our mermaid?"

"I don't know, exactly. But I'd like to think that they are. Thing is, though, that if you accidentally fall into the water, they'll capture you and take you to their world." He paused for effect. "And if you're there for more than three days, you can never return to land again."

"Why?" she asked, prodding him to finish the tale.

"Because they'll turn you into what they are, and you'll live in the water, becoming one of them."

She sighed, a bit dreamily. "Wouldn't it be cool if they were real, if you could really be transformed?"

"I went to Louisiana once with my parents, and when we visited the bayou, where my dad's ancestors were originally from, I kept wondering if the mermaids were there, watching us from below the water."

"I'll bet they were."

"I would've had to fall into the water to know for sure."

She moved closer to him. "I'm glad that you didn't or you wouldn't be here with me now."

He moved closer, as well. "Then I'm glad, too."

In the next bout of silence, they gazed at each other

as if they were the only two people on the island. At the moment, that was how it felt.

They finished their food, taking their final bites and putting their plates aside. For dessert, the guests would be making their own s'mores, and Jake was looking forward to watching Carol lick the chocolate and marshmallow off her lips.

"I think we should give her a name," she said.

"What?" He didn't have a clue what she was talking about. He was still thinking about her lips.

"The mermaid," she told him. "The one we made. She needs an identity before she gets washed away. Just to make her seem more real."

"Then you can choose one."

"It should probably be a French name since this area has so many French influences." She turned her attention to the sea. "Do you know how to say *ocean* in French?"

"It's *océan*." He pronounced it o-say-AHN. To the best of his knowledge, that was right. He wasn't an expert on the language, but he'd dated a French actress for a few whirlwind months. "I think that's actually a woman's name, too."

"Then it's perfect. She'll be Océan."

He smiled. "It definitely works."

"Yes, it does. When she's washed into the sea, she'll be dissolving into her name."

"What's the origin of your name?" This woman who was fueling his fantasies, he thought. His temporary lover.

"It's a song or a hymn."

"Oh, of course. That makes sense." He analyzed his own name. "Jacob means *supplanter* because, in the Bible, Jacob was born holding his twin brother's heel."

"I've never heard of that word."

"A supplanter takes the place of someone or something else."

"Really? Hmm. Who are you taking over for?"

"How about the kinds of guys you normally date?" He touched her cheek, skimming his finger across her skin.

Her breathing grew quiet. "That's a clever analogy. With how different you are from them."

He thought about how she sewed pieces of material together to document her life. "Are you going to make a quilt to mark this weekend?"

Her lashes fluttered. "Do you think I should?"

He nodded. "You can use fabrics with beachy things on them. An island, a mermaid, a sandcastle."

"What should I use to represent us?" she asked.

He trailed his hand down, following the line of her collarbone. "You could steal the sheets off my bed and cut them into little squares."

"Jake." She admonished him, but she shivered from his touch, too. "I'll figure something else out."

"Does that mean you're going to make the quilt?"

"I don't know." She seemed to be considering the idea, contemplating the design. "Maybe."

"You could give it to me as a gift."

"Really? You'd want it?"

"Sure." He toyed with the mesh on her cover-up, poking at the holes. "It can be a part of our secret after we get home. Something for us to remember being together."

She leaned toward him. "Wouldn't it be better for us to try to forget?"

In lieu of a response, he kissed her. For now, he didn't want to forget. She reacted favorably, her lips warm and pliable against his. After they separated, they sat back to watch the fire.

Jake glanced over and saw that the ingredients for the s'mores were being passed around. "Are you ready for dessert?"

She nodded, and soon they were engaged in making the sticky treats. He took the liberty of watching her eat hers, just as he'd wanted to do.

"Everyone is supposed to go crabbing later," he said. "If they want to," he added. No one had to do anything that didn't appeal to them.

"Tonight?" She didn't just lick the goo from her lips. She licked it from her fingers, too. "I thought we'd be doing that tomorrow morning on a boat."

"No. This is a nighttime activity. They're giant land crabs, so we'll be searching for them, going into the brush, along the inland trails, armed with flashlights. But we have to be quick and quiet, so we'll be splitting into separate groups once everyone gets the gist of it. So, do you want to join in?"

She nodded. "I'll give it a try. But it sounds sort of scary, being out there in the dark."

"I promise I'll protect you." He watched while she made herself another s'more. "We'll have to put on some warmer clothes. They'll be giving us gloves and buckets and whatever else we'll need. The caretakers of the house are going to be our guides."

"That's good." She focused on her task, placing her marshmallows just so. "But I'm going to stay close to you, for sure."

"That's not a problem." He wanted to keep her as close as possible. "I don't know how many we'll catch, but the island is supposed to be filled with them this time of year. The chef is going to incorporate our catch into the breakfast menu."

"I wish tomorrow wasn't our last day."

"Me, too." They would be flying out, just before sunset, and going back to their regular lives. But for now, they were still here, immersed in the romance that had become their affair.

Eight

This was it, Carol thought as she stood on her veranda, breathing in the tropical air. Soon, she and Jake would be leaving the Caribbean.

Already feeling nostalgic, she smiled, remembering last night's crabbing expedition. She'd squealed like a child when she'd nabbed her first giant blue crustacean. Jake had been right by her side, as promised, making the experience sweet and fun and romantic. Nonetheless, hunting and gathering wasn't her forte.

Eating was, though. She'd enjoyed the crab-stuffed crepes they'd had for breakfast. For lunch, they'd had French cuisine, served in the dining room, where everyone had gathered for their final meal, talking and laughing, before they'd parted ways.

Some guests were already gone by now and others, like Carol and Jake, were preparing to depart.

She returned to her room, where her suitcase sat, carefully packed. After Jake finished jamming his belongings into his, they would head out for the helipad. When they got to the other island where they'd originally landed, they would board the jet that would take them home.

She checked on Jake to see how he was coming along and found him looking as handsome as ever, dressed in blue jeans and a loose cotton shirt, with a shiny packet in his hand.

Carol gaped at him. "Where you did get that?" As far as she knew, they'd used the final condom last night, after they'd come back from crabbing and climbed in the tub together, taking a long sensual bath.

"It was in my luggage, but in a different compartment from where I usually keep them. It was lodged in the corner, so the edges are bent. But other than that…"

She caught her breath. "Do we have time to use it?"

"We'll make time." With lightning speed, he swept her into his arms. They kissed like crazy, tongue-to-tongue, instantly hungry for the forbidden taste of each other.

He backed her against a nightstand, and she opened his zipper and pushed her hand inside. His eyes went glassy as he pressed into her palm, letting her feel him up.

After a few anxious heartbeats, he went after her, lifting the hem of her soft summer dress and removing her panties. In the next frantic second, he shoved his jeans down and donned the protection.

Carol sat on the edge of the nightstand, and as he thrust into her, she locked her legs around him, pulling him closer.

"I like that you don't wear underwear," she told him.

"You should stop wearing it, too."

She couldn't fathom it, not in her daily life. "I'm too proper for that."

He nipped at her chin with his teeth, gently, wildly. "Yes, you should see how proper you look right now, with your dress hiked up around your hips."

Her bottom was getting sore from the friction of the wood beneath her, but she didn't care. "I couldn't find my panties on that first morning-after." But later she'd uncovered them, on the floor, with Jake's discarded clothes. Or more precisely, his pants, since that was the only thing he'd been wearing.

He pushed deeper, harder. "I should have kept them as a memento."

"So I could sew them into the quilt?"

He didn't stop the driving rhythm, not for an instant. "Patchwork panties. That works for me."

She still hadn't decided if she was going to make him a quilt. For now, all that mattered was being with him one more time.

He kissed her again, making the back of her throat hum. With her arms looped around his neck, she dug her nails into his shirt and arched her body toward his, taking as much of him as he was willing give.

Jake gave her everything. Rough and fast. Hot and sexy. Dark flashes of pleasure zinged through her blood. She closed her eyes, wanting this desperate moment to last forever, yet knowing it couldn't.

He used his fingers, rubbing her, intensifying the sensation. She was spiraling into sexual oblivion, lost in the fury. He ravished her relentlessly, lifting her into a fiery abyss.

Carol came in a burst of heat, in a sea of molten wetness. The air was thick, her breaths choppy.

He emitted a gritty groan, and all she could think was how beautiful he was, how powerfully male. His climax exploded just seconds after hers, expelling energy and lust.

She untangled her legs from around his waist, and he put his forehead against hers. In the aftermath, she clung to the feeling, her heart beating a crazy cadence.

When they separated, she wanted to pull him back into her arms. But she knew that wouldn't change anything. So she let him go.

While he went into the bathroom to clean up, she made a beeline to her own bathroom, grabbing her panties along the way. This time, she wasn't going to lose them in the shuffle.

Carol returned with her dress smooth and tidy, her underwear in place. Jake came back with his shirt tucked in and his fly neatly zipped.

Fighting a bout of sadness, she glanced down at her feet. She was wearing sandals decorated with little sparkling gems. The other jewels, the real ones Jake had given her, were packed. She didn't know if she would ever put them on again.

"Ready?" he asked.

She looked up at him. "To go home and act as if nothing happened?"

He nodded.

She searched his gaze, but all she saw, all she felt, were her own scattered emotions staring back at her. "I think I will make you a quilt, with all of the Caribbean trimmings."

"Promise?"

"Yes." She wanted Jake to remember that she'd once been his lover, even years from now, when she was happily married to someone else. "Just so you'll have it."

"Thanks. But we better go now." He took charge of the luggage, his and hers. "Should we ask the caretakers for a ride to the helipad or do you want to walk?"

"We can walk." It was a paved path, with stairs leading to the raised platform. "But I'd like to go the beach first, to the area where the sandcastle was. Or might still be." Even if it was in ruins, she wanted to see the remnants.

"Okay." He agreed to take her there.

They went downstairs, left their suitcases on the front porch and ventured onto the beach. But there was nothing to see. Everything was gone, including their beloved mermaid.

"We're too late," he said.

"Did the candles get washed away, too?" she asked, trying not to feel empty inside.

"I think someone removed them. I doubt Lena would have allowed them to pollute the ocean."

"That's good." Carol turned to look at him as a salty breeze skimmed the shore. "It's so quiet."

He captured a strand of her billowing hair. "Lena told me at lunch that she really likes you."

Carol leaned closer. "I like her, too." She'd gotten to know the pop star a little better. During the course of the weekend, they'd chatted here and there. But mostly Lena just smiled whenever she saw Jake and Carol together, saluting Carol for taking a sexy chance on him.

He released her hair, sliding it through his fingers. "And you were worried about fitting in with my friends."

"But I misbehaved like them instead?"

"Much to my pleasure." He kissed her, soft and slow, surrounded by the tropical paradise that helped inspire their affair.

Their last kiss, she thought. Their last moment. She slipped her arms around him, holding him as if it was never going to end. Only, they both knew it was coming to a close.

But still, she deepened the kiss, savoring the taste of him for as long as she could.

A little over a month had passed since the island trip, and now Jake was meeting Garrett for a drink at the LA-area resort Garrett owned. The main building was a grand hotel, with a view of the Pacific Ocean. To the west of it, along the boardwalk, were private condos. Guests could stay at either type of accommodation, depending on their needs.

On this crisp, clear afternoon, a group of people were horseback riding along the shore. Garrett was a horseman who'd built a fancy stable on the property for himself as much as for his guests. In fact, he lived on the premises, near the stables, in a custom-built house on a cliff above the beach.

Jake entered the hotel, his thoughts scattered. He was supposed to be concentrating on a fund-raiser that was in the works for their foundation, but he kept thinking about Carol instead.

She'd called in sick four times this week. That wasn't like her. She rarely, if ever, missed work. She did seem ill, though. The last time he'd seen her, she looked tired and pale. But Jake wasn't sure if it was physical or emotional.

Being around each other was becoming increasingly difficult, even with the amount of time that had passed since Lena's party. They did the best they could, but it was awkward, with both of them overcompensating for the heat that still sizzled between them. He wasn't sure what was worse: being alone at the office with her or having other people around. Either way, he was feeling the pressure, and so was she.

Was it the stress that was making her sick? He wouldn't be surprised if it was. But at this point he didn't know what to do about it other than urge her to see a doctor, if she hadn't done that already.

He was concerned that if it continued for much longer she was going to find herself another job, one that didn't include an ex-lover as her boss.

Then what would he do? How would he replace her? Carol was an asset to his company…and to him. She understood him. She knew what made him tick. But maybe it would be better if she left, if they didn't have to see each other every day. No, he thought. He didn't want to lose her, not like this.

"Hey! Where are you going?"

Jake spun around and saw that he'd just walked right past Garrett in the front lobby bar. Cripes, he didn't even realize what he was doing.

"Sorry. I just—" Rather than try to explain, Jake finished with, "Need a beer."

"Me, too." Garrett motioned to a table that had been reserved for them.

They sat down, and a spunky little blonde came by to take their orders. They both chose bottled Mexican beer. Normally, Jake would have checked out the waitress or at least smiled at her in his usual flirtatious way, but he was too preoccupied with thoughts of Carol to behave like his old self. Garrett seemed the same as usual, except maybe a bit more uptight.

Not that he was a stick in the mud. Garrett Snow was a great guy, just in a strong-willed way. He didn't take any crap from anyone, and he didn't party or play the field the way Jake did, either. Garrett had always been a one-woman kind of man. He was also organized and focused. He preferred to do things himself, barely needing a secretary or assistant. Jake couldn't fathom it. Carol was the most important person in his employ.

The beers arrived and Jake swigged his first. He glanced around, taking in the decor, with its rich, dark woods, painted details and Native American accents. Garrett was a mixed-blood from the Cheyenne Nation, sired by an Anglo father he'd never known.

"You look like you have a lot on your mind," Garrett said, reaching for his beer.

"Yeah, I do. I don't know if I'm going to be much good today, finalizing the fund-raiser stuff."

Garrett sat back in his chair. He was tall and broad, with deep-set eyes, short black hair and hard-edged features. He squinted a lot, just as he was doing now. "We can work on it another day."

"Really?" Jake was surprised. His foster brother rarely pushed business aside. "You'd be cool with that?"

"I have things on my mind, too."

Curious, Jake leaned forward. "Like what?"

Garrett didn't respond. He didn't alter his posture, either. He remained as he was, seated far back in his chair, his eyes narrowed. He looked like the hero of an old Western B movie, a half-breed cowboy, preparing to fight the bad guys and clean up the town.

Finally he said, "The woman who ripped us off will be coming up for parole this year."

Ah, so that was it, Jake thought. Garrett had Meagan Quinn on his mind. The seemingly nice girl who'd embezzled money from them. She used to work for the accounting firm that Garrett, Max and Jake used, gaining access to their financial records and dipping her hands into the pie.

Jake was the most forgiving, of course. He knew what it was like to steal. "She's serving her time. She's paying her debt to society."

"Yes, but she still has to pay her debt to us."

That was true. As a stipulation of her sentence, Meagan had been ordered to pay restitution to her victims. The money she'd taken wasn't an astronomical amount, at least not by their standards. But it was still a crime. And it had still pissed them off, especially Garrett, maybe even more than it should have.

Jake took another swig of his beer. "Doesn't she have to get a verified job offer before she can get paroled? Isn't that one of the terms of her release?"

"Yeah, and my do-gooder mother wants me to offer her a job, here at the resort."

Holy cow. If Jake hadn't been so shocked, he might've laughed. Regardless, he still cracked a joke. "Doing what? Working the front desk so she can get your guests' credit card numbers and go on a shopping spree?"

"That isn't funny."

"Yes, it is. I mean, seriously, what the hell is your mom thinking?"

"She's thinking that I'll be able to give an ex-con a fresh start at a new life. Of course, the parole commission would have to approve her working for me, but since the restitution she owes would be going to our foundation, they'd probably agree to it."

Jake nodded. An arrangement had already been made with the court for the money to be donated to their charity, instead of being paid to them. Garrett had taken care of that when he'd attended Meagan's sentencing. Neither Jake nor Max had made an appearance. They'd trusted Garrett to represent them.

"Mom's got it in her head that I *need* to do this, as much for the thief as myself."

"A little forgiveness wouldn't hurt."

"Yeah, well, we'll see." Garrett chugged his drink, then set the bottle down with a thud. After a moment of silence, he asked, "So what's going on with you?"

Well, shit. Now Jake had to spill his guts, too. Only, he couldn't admit that he'd slept with Carol. He'd promised to keep their affair on the down-low once they got home, and that included not blabbing to his foster brothers about it.

"I'm just worried about Carol," he said.

Garrett's expression softened. "Your assistant? How so?"

"She's been sick this week."

A frown appeared on Garrett's face. "How sick?"

"I don't know. She just seems run-down, I guess."

"Then give her some time to recover."

"Maybe I should stop by her place to check on her."

"Sure, you could do that. But you should probably call first."

"Or text," Jake said, recalling the texts that had led to their first night together. "I just want to know that she's going to be okay."

"You're really reliant on her, aren't you?"

"She's good at her job." Hot and sexy in bed, too, he thought. And warm and sweet. Everything he wasn't supposed to be thinking about. But he couldn't seem to let those images go, no matter how hard he tried. "I'll text her after I finish my beer."

"I'm getting another one." Garrett lifted his empty bottle and signaled the waitress.

Jake wasn't having another drink. He wanted to keep a clear head for when he saw Carol.

Jake rang Carol's doorbell and shifted the bag in his hand. In his text, he'd offered to bring her some soup. It was as good an excuse as any to con his way over here. Besides, he knew how much she loved the matzo ball soup from a nearby deli.

She answered the door, looking even more exhausted than the last time he'd seen her at work. Dang, he thought. He'd hoped that her condition would be improving, not worsening.

After she invited him inside, he held up the soup. "Do you want this now?"

"Maybe a little. Thank you." Carol took the bag and went into the kitchen. Jake waited at the entrance of the kitchen, watching her move about. She opened the container and poured some of the broth into a mug, then spooned a matzo ball into it. "There's a lot here. Do you want a cup, too?"

"No, thanks." Jake studied her more closely. She was wearing sweatpants and a blousy shirt, and her typically tidy hair was pulled up into a rooster-style pony-tail, the ends poking out at feathery angles. In a more relaxed situation, the chaotic style would have amused him. But he was in no mood to smile.

She motioned to the living room, and he followed her to the sofa, where he sat beside her.

She tasted the soup. "It's really good. Thank you again."

"You're welcome." He paused before he continued, giving her time to eat a bit more of the soup. Then he asked, "Have you seen a doctor yet?"

She shook her head. "I wanted to wait until…"

Jake frowned. "Until what?"

"I was ready."

That made absolutely no sense to him. "You've been sick for almost a week."

"I'll make an appointment if I need to."

"I think you need to now."

She put her mug on the coffee table. "Let me handle my own business, Jake."

"I'm just worried is all."

"I'll be fine."

She didn't look fine. Not in the least. He'd never seen her in such a fragile state before.

"I started on the quilt I promised to make for you," she said, changing the subject. "But it's slow going."

"You've been sewing?"

"No. But I cut the squares from the different fabrics. Or most of them. I still need to order a few more." She glanced toward a basket in the corner of the room where the fabrics were. "You can look at what's there so far, if you want."

He went ahead and checked it out, curious to see what patterns she'd chosen. But that didn't mean he was going to let her get away with ignoring her health issues. He intended to work their conversation back to that. But first, he retrieved the basket and brought it over to the sofa.

He looked through the squares. There were a variety of fabrics, most of them containing the beach themes he'd suggested, with depictions of mermaids, sand-castles and islands on them. She'd even tossed in some printed with blue crabs. There was also a multicolored print that had the same jewel tones as the bracelet he'd given her. She'd included a shiny starfish pattern for the earrings, too. He noticed a geometric Native American print as well, that he assumed was meant to represent him and his heritage. He kept looking and uncovered a stack of squares with grasshoppers on them.

"For Eskeilay," she said. Then softly added, "The mother of the earth-womb."

"You did a beautiful job with what you chose." He wished that he could touch her, hold her, make her feel better, but he figured the last thing she wanted was for him to take her in his arms.

"I plan to include something for Uncta, too. A fire print of some sort, something with a golden hue. That's one of the fabrics I still have to order."

"I appreciate your attention to detail." To the memories they'd created, even if neither of them had spoken of that weekend since.

"I don't know when I'll finish it."

To him, it sounded as if she had mixed feelings about whether to complete it at all. She'd probably only brought it up as a diversion to keep him from bugging her about going to the doctor.

Jake put the basket aside, refusing to let her off the hook. He asked, "Are you ill because of me?"

She had a worried expression. "What?"

He clarified his question. "Is being around me too stressful?"

She twisted her hands on her lap. "Sort of, I guess. Not wanting to face you is part of the reason I've been calling in sick."

"You're facing me now. You agreed to let me come over."

"I knew I couldn't avoid you forever. And it is a little easier seeing you here than at the office. But I still don't want to talk about it. Not until I see a doctor, and I already told you, I'm not ready to do that."

He pushed the issue, determined to get answers. "Please, Carol, just tell me what's going on."

"It's too soon to tell you."

"Too soon for what?" He noticed that she was still wringing her hands. "I'm not leaving here until you level with me."

Her breath rushed out. "Okay, but it's going to freak

you out." She looked directly at him, her voice quaver-
ing. "I'm scared, Jake. Scared to death that I might be
pregnant."

Nine

Carol waited for Jake to respond. But he just sat there staring at her. Was he struggling to grasp what she'd just told him? Or was he simply too stunned to move? To blink? To talk?

After what seemed like forever, he said, "That's impossible."

"In what way?" she asked, prodding him to explain what he was thinking and feeling.

"We used protection." He spoke robotically, like a computer stating a fact. Or someone who refused to believe what he was hearing.

"Condoms sometimes fail." She'd checked the failure rates and the numbers were staggering. "Mostly from them breaking or slipping off."

"But that didn't happen to us."

"No, but I might have damaged the first one. With as much as I fumbled with it, I could have poked a tiny hole in it. Or the failure could have come from the last one we used. Remember how the edges of the packet were bent from the way it had been stuck in your suitcase? The condom itself could have been compromised without us even knowing it."

Jake stood and stepped away from the sofa, pressing his back against the fireplace mantel. He was beginning to look like a caged animal. Carol knew exactly how he felt.

"Then I guess it is possible," he said.

"Yes, it is." Her voice vibrated with every breath she took. She'd never expected to be in this position, possibly impregnated by a man who didn't want children. "Last week, I thought I had my period, but it was weird. First of all, it was early and that's never happened to me before." Normally her cycles were like clockwork. "And it only lasted a few hours, which was even weirder." She hated to share all of the clinical details, but considering how crucial this was, it seemed necessary. "It was more like spotting than a full period."

"I'm confused." His voice was shaky, too. He even cleared his throat, as if it might help. "That isn't an early sign of pregnancy, is it?"

"Actually, it is. But I wasn't aware of it until I looked up my symptoms online. At first I thought I was getting a virus based on how run-down I was feeling. Then when my period seemed irregular, I got a little worried and researched what could've caused that. And that's when I came across something called implantation bleeding. It's just like what I had. It's a result of the fertilized egg attaching itself to the wall of the uterus. It typically happens two to seven days before the beginning of what would be your regular menstrual cycle. In my case, it's been about six days. My period is due tomorrow."

He looked relieved—not completely, but at least his body language wasn't quite as tense. "Then maybe it'll start and everything will be okay. Maybe you'll begin to feel better, too."

"That's what I'm hoping. That's why I didn't want to take a pregnancy test or go to a doctor yet, either."

He wrinkled his forehead. "Can a test even be taken this early?"

Carol nodded. "Yes, but I wanted to wait, just to see if my period comes first. Besides, early tests aren't always accurate." She reached for her soup, needing fuel, so she cut into the matzo ball and ate a portion of that. "I haven't been queasy, so that's a good sign. Mostly my symptoms are lack of energy and light-headedness. It might just be stress. Sometimes women's menstrual cycles can get disrupted by that."

He relaxed a bit more, moving away from the mantel. "Then that's probably what it is. It seems the most likely culprit. Even I figured that's what was wrong with you and why you're not feeling well. That's why I came over here to question you about it."

"I appreciate your concern." She hadn't wanted to

see him until after she knew for sure, but she was glad that she'd gotten it over with. "If my cycle starts tomorrow, we're in the clear. But if it doesn't…"

He tugged at his hair, hard enough to create a grimace. "Pregnancy never even occurred to me."

"Me, neither, until all of this blew up in my face." She wanted to pull her hair out, too.

"If you don't start your period, how long are you going to wait before you take a test?"

"I don't know. A few days, maybe. I don't want to sit around on pins and needles, but I don't want to get a false reading, either." She was just hoping and praying that her cycle showed up. "I could go to the doctor to get a blood test. Those give you an earlier reading. But it takes longer to get the results than a urine test, so I'd have to wait, either way. I doubt my doctor would rush the results of a blood test for me."

"Will you call me tomorrow and let me know how you're doing and if anything happens?"

"Of course I will." Now that he was part of the equation, she would keep him well informed. "But if you hadn't come over today, I wouldn't have told you any of this, not until enough time passed for me to be sure." She blinked, fighting back tears. "I didn't want to worry you if it turned out to be nothing." She put down her soup, leaving the spoon inside the mug. "I'm so scared, Jake."

"Me, too." He resumed his seat on the sofa, looking at her as if she might break. "But it'll be okay."

She wished that she could believe him. But what if

she was pregnant? He was the last man on earth she should be having a baby with. "You can't know it's going to be okay."

"I'm just trying to comfort you. To say what I'm supposed to say." Clearly, he was struggling with his role in this. "Would you rather be alone now? Do you want me to leave?"

She looked into the vastness of his eyes. "Do you want to go?"

He gazed back at her. "I asked you first."

They sounded like kids, debating a silly subject. But that wasn't the case. This was a serious discussion between two anxiety-ridden adults.

She took the undecided road. "It's up to you."

"Please, Carol. Either ask me to stay or tell me to leave. Don't make me choose."

"Then maybe you should go." If he stayed, she might fall prey to the temptation of those big broad shoulders and put her head on one of them. She might even cry in his arms, and that wouldn't do either of them any good.

"All right." He wiped his hands on his pants, as if his palms had turned clammy. "We'll just keep in touch by phone."

She walked him to the door, where they both stood outside. The air felt good, so she breathed in as much of it as she could.

"Take care of yourself," he said.

"I will." She hadn't been sleeping. She'd barely even been eating. "Thanks again for the soup."

"If you need anything else, just let me know."

What she needed was to *not* be pregnant. "Hopefully you'll get good news from me tomorrow."

"I'll be waiting." He gazed empathetically at her. "I'm sorry our weekend together is messing up your life."

"Nothing is messed up yet." It was only on the verge of disaster.

His breathing turned choppy. "God, Carol. How are we going to handle this if it's true?"

"I don't know. But you need to go." She couldn't cope with his panic. She had enough of her own.

"You're right. I'm sorry. I'm supposed to be leaving."

Thankfully, he didn't embrace her or do anything to stir up more emotion. There was nothing but a softly spoken goodbye before he turned and left.

She noticed that he was driving his Corvette, a ragtop convertible that he favored on warmer days. She could see the shiny red sports car from where she stood. She watched him climb behind the wheel and fire up the high-powered engine.

Carol tried to picture him in a minivan with a baby carrier strapped in the backseat, but it was a ludicrous image.

She shook her head, afraid, so damned afraid, that if tomorrow didn't bring an end to this, her wild-spirited boss could actually be the father of her unborn child.

Nearly a week later, Jake was at home stressing about the predicament he'd gotten himself into. Carol hadn't returned to work yet, but by now a doctor had confirmed what the home test had also revealed. She was pregnant. With his kid, Jake thought. His flesh and blood. He was going to be someone's dad.

Carol had already told him over the phone that she was keeping it, but he'd figured as much. He couldn't see her terminating her pregnancy under any circumstances, not with how badly she wanted a family.

But how did Jake fit into all of this? He didn't know how to be part of a family, not since he'd lost his own. Nor did he want to be part of one, either.

Carol was coming over later so they could try to figure things out. But even now, as he looked at himself in the mirrored wall of his gym, he wanted to ram his head against it.

He'd worked out like mad, making his muscles ache, making his body sweat. He'd pushed himself harder than he ever had before, trying to block the truth from his mind.

But it hadn't been the least bit effective.

What the hell was he going to do? How was he going to cope with being a father? Jake didn't even have a dog. Or a cat. Or a fish. He'd never been responsible for anyone or anything except himself.

He entered the bathroom that was attached to the gym and climbed into the shower. He turned on the spigot and let the icy cold water pummel him. But it didn't help. Nothing did. Still, he remained under the freezing spray for as long as he could stand it.

After he toweled off, he dragged a T-shirt over his head and zipped into a pair of holey jeans. He liked wearing old clothes around the house. For him, it took the pretentious edge off living in a mansion. Not that he was complaining. His place was amazingly cool, an ultramodern estate perched in the Hollywood Hills, with the kinds of amenities only high-dollar real estate could offer.

At least Jake could buy his son or daughter everything the child needed. That was his only comfort, the only part of this that made him feel grounded.

Over the years, he'd learned to hide behind his money. But if he hadn't gotten rich, he would be hiding behind something else. There would be a barrier either way. On the day Jake's family had burned to death in that car, he'd put up his defenses, using his grief as a shield. There was no going back, no changing it. He was what he was.

He went into the living room to wait for Carol, anxiety building with each second that passed. He couldn't marry her; he couldn't be the nice normal guy she dreamed about. But she wouldn't expect him to. Would she?

He scrubbed his hand across his jaw, feeling trapped within the walls of his big glass house.

Finally, Carol arrived. He invited her inside, and they sat across from each other in his sunken living room, decorated with red leather furniture and sleek gray tables. The floors were high-glossed wood, the artwork bold and masculine. The windows offered panoramic views, with Hollywood and all its glorious sins stretched out before them. This wasn't a home designed for a wife and child. He'd bought it as a place to party, to entertain, to live and let live.

"Can I get you anything?" he asked. "Water? Iced tea? Wine?" He stalled, made a face. Had he just offered a pregnant woman a drink? "Sorry. Scratch the wine."

"That's okay. I don't want anything, anyway."

Carol looked prim and pretty, with her oxford blouse all buttoned up. But she seemed tired, too. As fatigued as before.

"Has the nausea started?" he asked.

She shook her head. "No. My symptoms are the same."

"Maybe you won't get sick like that."

She smiled a little. "I probably will, but it would be nice to bypass that part."

"I don't know anything about having kids, Carol."

"I'm not an expert, either."

"Yeah, but it's in your DNA. You're going to make a great mom."

"Thank you. This wasn't how I envisioned becoming a parent, but I'm not going to let that stop me from loving this baby with all of my heart."

At that moment, Jake's heart was beating uncomfortably in his chest, crushing down on his lungs. "I'll give you both whatever you need. Neither of you will go without. But I can't marry you, Carol. I hope you understand that."

"Of course I do. I didn't come over here hoping for a proposal. I could never marry you, either."

He should have been satisfied with her response. It was what he wanted to hear, after all. But instead, it made him hurt for the child they'd created. Oddly enough, he hurt for himself and Carol, too.

"I'll buy you a house," he said. "Around here some-where. Then at least we can live close enough for me to see the kid regularly, too. I can come over and tuck it into bed or whatever."

She bit down on her bottom lip. "Oh, wow. Jake."

He frowned. "Oh, wow, what?"

Her eyes turned a little misty. "You're already start-ing to sound like a dad."

"I am?" He didn't feel like one. All he felt was sad and scared and confused. Not knowing what else to say, he went silent, hoping she didn't go into a full-blown cry.

Thankfully, she cleared the mistiness, blinking it away. Then she said, "I appreciate your offer. But you don't have to buy me a house."

"I'm in real estate. Investing in property is what I do." So why wouldn't he want to make an investment for her, too? "Besides, you can't stay in the apartment. It's too small for you and the baby."

"Okay, but maybe you can keep the house in your name, instead of gifting it to me. I want to be my own person and taking too much from you doesn't feel right."

He wasn't going to argue with her, not in her condi-tion. He would abide by her wishes for now. "You can at least pick out the kind of place you like."

"I don't want it to be too big." She glanced around at his enormous digs. "I'd prefer something a little homier, you know?"

"That's fine." There were plenty of bungalows in the hills, with the warmth and charm of a family dwelling, which was what he figured she was after. "We'll find something that suits you."

"There's no rush. I can stay at my apartment until closer to when the baby comes." She placed a hand on her stomach, splaying her fingers across it, making him reflect on the little life that grew there. "We still have a long time to go."

"There's no point in waiting until the end." Jake considered how the tables had turned. Normally Carol insisted on getting things done ahead of time, but now he was the one trying to make early arrangements. He didn't know what had come over him, jumping into this the way he was. Maybe it was because she seemed so lost?

"What are we going to do about my job?" she asked.

"What do you mean?"

"Am I supposed to keep working for you? And when are we going to tell the people at the office?"

"Of course you can keep working for me." He'd already been worried about losing her before he even knew she was pregnant. He most certainly didn't want her to leave him now. "And we can arrange a meeting at the office and tell everyone at the same time. We'll just say it, plain and simple."

"It makes me nervous."

"I know." His stomach was in knots. "But it's better to just get it over with." He didn't want anyone figuring things out on their own or spreading gossip. "We'll control it ourselves, if we can."

"Will you handle that? I don't think I have the strength to stand in a room in front of my peers and admit that I slept with you."

"Yes, I'll handle it. And don't worry. I'm not going to go into the specifics. This is about the baby, not about what we did."

She kept her hand on her stomach. "Kristen is going to be concerned about me. You know how she is."

Kristen was the receptionist, a pixie-haired brunette in her early twenties who followed Carol around like a puppy. Jake had never really bonded with the girl. It was Carol she was loyal to. Kristen was filling in for Carol while she was out sick, doing what she could to assist Jake and make Carol proud. "She admires you."

"I know. I like her, too. But I never expected to be in this position. It seems so surreal."

"We'll get through it," he said, even if he didn't have a clue how they were going to manage having a child together for the rest of their lives. "As soon as you're ready to return to the office, I'll call that meeting."

"I'll come back on Friday."

That was two days away. "Then that's when it'll happen." When Jake would announce that he and Carol were having a baby. When the news would be official. When their mixed-up future would begin.

* * *

The Friday meeting was awkward, but at least it was over. Carol wasn't going to have to lie about why she wasn't feeling well. Or hide her baby bump when it started to appear. Or stress about when to tell everyone at work. As of this morning, they already knew.

Jake had handled it like the boss he was, stating only the facts. He'd made it clear that he and Carol weren't in a relationship. He explained that they would raise their child in separate households. He also pointed out that she would continue to work for him, so it would be business as usual.

Yeah, right, Carol thought. As if it was just that easy.

After the meeting ended, the other employees disbursed, silence looming in the air as they filed out of the conference room. Carol understood their discomfort. She was feeling out of sorts, too. But she suspected that Kristen was going to approach her privately, as soon as the eager receptionist was able to swing it.

Jake went to his office, and Carol headed to hers, glad to escape. She sat at her desk, trying to pull herself into work mode.

About an hour later, a light knock sounded at her open doorway. Sure enough, it was Kristen, with her trendy clothes, short, cutesy hair and big hoop earrings. Carol gestured for her to come inside.

Kristen entered the room and closed the door behind her. Then she widened her eyes and said, "Oh, my freaking God. You're going to be Jake's baby mama.

You! The nicest, most normal woman on the planet. I can't believe it."

Carol could hardly believe it, either. "Things happen."

"I'll say." Kristen sighed. "I always wondered if you had feelings for him, though."

"You did?" And here Carol thought that she'd hidden her crush on Jake without anyone figuring it out.

The brunette nodded. She was a petite young woman who'd played Peter Pan in a community play. She toyed around with acting, but lots of people in LA dabbled in the arts. Kristen wasn't overly ambitious about it. Mostly she was just a flighty girl who'd gone from one bad boyfriend to another. Carol had helped her through her last horrific relationship.

"At least Jake has lots of money," Kristen said. "At least he can take care of the baby that way. But dang, it's hard to envision him being an actual dad."

Carol thought about what Jake had said about tucking the child in at night and how emotional it had made her feel. "I think he's going to try to do his best."

"That's good. My parents weren't married or anything, either. I hardly ever saw my dad when I was kid. I see him even less now."

"I'm sorry your dad hasn't taken a more active role in your life." No doubt it had factored into Kristen's terrible taste in men, too. "That wasn't fair to you."

"What happened to you and Jake when you were kids wasn't fair, either. At least my parents are still alive. But it's still so weird, with you and Jake having a baby together."

"He offered to put me up in a house near his to make it easier for him to get involved. But this isn't how I ever imagined raising a child."

"I'm just glad it's you and not one of his hoity-toity ex-girlfriends having his kid. You're a genuine person, and you'll be a great mom."

"Thank you. Jake said the same thing."

"About you being a good mom?"

"Yes. He thinks it's in my DNA." But regardless of what a natural mom she was going to be, Carol couldn't bear the thought of Jake being with other women. Yet once the dust settled, she suspected that he would dive back into his playboy ways. He was making a commitment to their child, not to her. "I just hope I don't break down before the baby is born."

"You won't. You're too strong to fall apart."

"I haven't cried yet." She'd gotten close, but she'd managed to keep from bursting into tears. "I'm trying to hold on."

"Don't worry. You'll make it." The receptionist sent her an encouraging smile. "But I better get back to work now."

"Thank you for the support."

"Sure. Should I leave the door open when I leave?"

Carol nodded, and once she was alone, she struggled to maintain her composure. Then she glanced up and saw Jake looming in the doorway. The hits just kept on coming, she thought.

"Are you okay?" he asked. "I noticed that Kristen was just here." He moved forward and closed the door, just as Kristen had done.

She tried to reassure him. "Everything is fine. She just wanted to talk."

"Did it help?"

Yes and no, Carol thought. Kristen's belief in her felt good, but thinking about Jake with other women had only heightened her duress.

"It was fine," she said again.

He didn't look convinced. "You can go home early if you need to."

"I'd rather stay." She didn't want to appear cowardly, skipping out on the first day.

Jake nodded and loosened his tie. He'd worn a proper suit to the meeting. His jacket was already gone, though. But he never remained in professional attire for too long, routinely discarding what he considered the stuffy portions of his wardrobe. Only, at the moment, his restless nature seemed even more pronounced.

He said, "No one has come to me to talk about it."

"Why would they? You're the boss."

"Who knocked up his assistant? I'll bet they think I took full advantage of you." He frowned. "I didn't do that, did I, Carol?"

The guilt in his eyes unnerved her. "No, you didn't, and me getting pregnant doesn't change the facts. I wanted you as badly as you wanted me." She'd made him well aware of that when they were in the midst of it, and she wasn't going to let him twist things up now. "Even Kristen said that she suspected I was attracted to you."

"Really? I guess women are observant that way. Of course, with the way she admires you, she would notice, I guess." He removed his tie and crammed it in his pants pocket. "I'm glad you're back. I missed having you around here."

"You're probably going to be seeing a lot of me outside of the office, too."

"Yeah." He smiled a little. "I've been trying to picture you months from now." He made a big-belly motion. "I've never touched a pregnant woman's stomach before."

Would he be touching hers? The thought made her weak. "I have. Lots of my girlfriends have kids."

"Have you told any of them yet?"

She shook her head. "I wanted to wait until everyone at work knew. I wanted to get that over with first." She questioned him. "Have you told Garrett or Max?"

"No. Max is still backpacking all over the country or whatever the hell he's doing. And since he's trying to stay off the grid, I'm going to wait to call him until the time feels right. But I'm going to tell Garrett this weekend. I already told him that you were sick, so now I can clarify why."

"I wonder what he'll think."

"After he gets over the initial shock, he'll probably want to kick my ass for not being more careful."

"It could have happened to anyone."

"Yeah, but it happened to me. The guy who plays

around. That won't go over well." He shoved the tie deeper into his pocket. "Are you nervous about telling your friends?"

"Yes." She couldn't deny that her news was going to worry them, too. "They're not going to like the idea of me being a single mom, not with how marriage-minded I've always been."

"I'm sorry, Carol."

For insisting that he couldn't marry her? "It's not a problem." She'd agreed with his reasoning from the beginning. "I know better than to think that having a baby is going to turn us into a lifelong couple."

"I wonder if it's going to be a boy or a girl."

"It's too early to tell. But we can find out during a midpregnancy ultrasound, if we want to know. They can't always tell for sure, though. It depends on the position the baby is in."

He kept looking at her, almost as if she was still his warm and willing lover. "I guess we'll cross that bridge when we come to it."

She shuffled a stack of papers on her desk, wishing he would stop intensifying their chemistry, especially when she was struggling to ignore it. "We have a lot of bridges to cross."

"Too many," he said, before he moved toward the door. "Do you want me to grab you some lunch later?"

Normally she got his lunch, if he wasn't dining out with clients. "No, thanks. But it was nice of you to ask."

"Okay, well… I'll see you."

"You, too." Was it crazy for her to wish that they

were right for each other? That he was a different type of man than he was? Probably. But she couldn't help it.

Somewhere in the pit of her dreamy soul, Carol wished that they were meant to be together like expectant parents should be.

Ten

Jake met with Garrett on the boardwalk located near the resort. They sat on a bright white bench, in front of a gourmet coffee shop that faced the ocean.

With as much strength as Jake could muster, he told his foster brother about the baby. As expected, the conversation wasn't going in his favor.

"It just happened," Jake said in his own defense.

"Earthquakes just happen. Tidal waves just happen." Garrett gestured to the water as if it was going to rise up like a monster and swallow them whole. "But getting your assistant pregnant? That could've been prevented."

Jake used the only excuse he could think of. "The condoms failed."

"You know that wasn't what I meant."

"Yeah, I know." Clearly, Garrett was suggesting that he should've never taken Carol to bed. "But I'm already a mess over it. So I'd prefer not to have you jumping all over me, too."

"I'm sorry, bro. I don't want to make this more difficult for you. But it's just that you got yourself into something major here. And Carol is a nice girl who shouldn't be left holding the bag."

"I'm trying to do right by her and the baby. I'm going to set them up in a place in my neighborhood and be there when they need me." Jake watched a family playing on the beach. The youngest kid was a fair-haired toddler, a rough-and-tumble boy squirming in his mom's arms. "I don't really know how, though. To be there, I mean."

"Just give it some time. You'll learn."

"I hope so. I want to keep her and the baby safe." He kept watching the family. The older kids were running toward the shore with their paddleboards, and the little one remained on his mom's lap; only now, he was playing with a red plastic bucket his dad had given him.

Garrett said, "Life takes some strange turns."

"Boy, does it ever." Being at the beach was making Jake miss the romance he'd had with Carol. But getting reinvolved with her in that way would only complicate things further. "I wonder if I should invite her to stay with me until we find her a house. Not as my lover or anything," he clarified. "But just so I can get more familiar with her pregnancy. So I can be part of it, too."

Garrett encouraged him. "That sounds like a solid idea to me."

"Maybe I'll take her on a picnic or something to-morrow and we can talk about it then." Unless she had plans on Sunday. He didn't have a clue what Carol did with her free time. "It's hard to say how she'll feel about it, though."

As Jake contemplated his all-too-grown-up life, a group of teenage girls walked by, checking out a cluster of boys who were seated on a brick wall. Typical of this generation, the girls were tapping away on their phones, probably announcing their flirtations on social media and sneaking in pictures of the boys, who were on their phones, too.

"So have you figured out what to do?" he asked Garrett.

"About what?"

"Offering Meagan Quinn a job."

"No, I haven't." Garrett seemed oblivious to the teen antics. Or maybe he just didn't care to notice them. "But there's plenty of time to decide. Her parole eligibility date is still months away. Then once that rolls around, there'll be a hearing. After that, her case will go into review. Her release isn't going to happen overnight."

"If she doesn't have a job lined up, she won't be re-leased. The parole commission isn't going to let that slide."

"I know. I'm considering how much weight an offer from me would hold." Garrett frowned. "Meagan has a child. A daughter, who'll be around two by the time Meagan gets out."

"She has a kid that age?" Jake was flabbergasted. "How is that even possible? She's been behind bars longer than that."

"She discovered that she was pregnant soon after she went to prison, by a guy who'd already walked out on her. She gave birth while she was incarcerated, and one of her brothers took care of the baby so it didn't have to go into foster care."

Jake hadn't been aware of Meagan's plight. "Have you been keeping tabs on her all this time?"

"No. I haven't paid her any mind while she's been locked up. I didn't even know that she'd had a kid until Mom told me, just recently. She just found out, too, when she took an interest in Meagan's parole."

"Damn. Your mother is really vested in this thing." Jake considered the circumstances. "I can't imagine someone having a baby in prison." The thought twisted his stomach, especially now that Carol was carrying his child.

Garrett squinted in the sun. "You know what else Mom discovered from poking around into Meagan's life? That she and Meagan's mother used to belong to the same Native American women's group. It was a long time ago, and their paths only crossed for a short period, but there's still a connection. Of course Mom thinks it's a sign, even if she barely knew the other woman."

"What happened to Meagan's mom?"

"She died before any of this went down."

"So she never saw her daughter get locked up? That's good, I guess. But it's sad, too, that she's dead." Jake knew what losing family was like. "Your resort would be a good place for Meagan to work, especially with the day care you built for your employees."

"Are you suggesting I should hire her because of that? Her child isn't my responsibility."

No, but from the tone in Garret's voice, Jake could tell that he was concerned about the kid. "With everything Meagan has been through, she may have been reformed."

"And maybe she hasn't changed a bit. She could be the same greedy little thief who ripped us off."

"You won't know unless you give her a chance. Besides, you don't really know what prompted her to take the money."

"Is there a good reason to steal?"

"No, but sometimes it's not about being greedy. I started stealing to try to fill the hole where my heart used to be. Then later, I did it to impress the girls I was with. You remember how messed up I was then."

"Yes, I remember. We were all a mess in those days." Garrett blew out a breath. "I still don't know what I'm going to do. But at least I have some time to think about it."

"I've got a lot to think about, too." Jake shifted his attention back to the family on the beach, where the toddler had been handed over to his dad, so his mom could pour apple juice in his tippy cup or sippy cup or whatever it was called.

Jake was definitely going to ask Carol to stay with him for a while and try to figure things out. But whether or not she accepted the invitation was a whole other matter.

On Sunday, Carol met with Jake at a park in her neighborhood. When he'd called to ask her to join him for a picnic, he'd told her that he wanted to discuss another aspect of the baby arrangement. She wasn't sure what that meant exactly. But she understood that there was still plenty to talk about. So here she was, waiting to see what he had to say.

They shared a blanket beneath a big, shady tree, with a cooler of food that Jake's chef had prepared.

"So what's on your mind?" she asked.

He filled his plate. "Maybe we can relax a bit before we get into the specifics?"

"All right." She allowed him the luxury he'd requested, even if she was impatient to know what had triggered this meeting. "It's a nice park. I've never been here before."

"Me, neither." He glanced around. "It's busy today."

Carol nodded. There was even a group who'd gathered for a family reunion, with homemade signs leading to their get-together. "Lots of people are barbecuing."

"My family used to grill in our backyard. The whole suburban weekend thing."

"Did your dad do the cooking?"

"Yes. But Mom always got everything ready ahead of time, and then he would get credit for how good it was."

Carol turned nostalgic. "It was like that at our house, too." It was also the type of lifestyle she'd always envisioned having. But this wasn't the time to think about that, not while she was pregnant with Jake's baby.

He said, "I don't like doing things my family used to do. It just makes me miss them more."

She sighed. "It helps me to remember mine."

"You and I are different in that way."

"We're different in lots of ways." They'd known it from the day they'd met, and now they were bringing a child into the world.

He ate a handful of grapes. "How often are you supposed to see the doctor?"

She spread a dollop of Brie cheese on a sliced pear. "Once a month, until I'm further along. Then it'll be every two weeks. After that, it'll be every week until the baby comes."

"I wonder if you'll have any food cravings."

She savored the pear. "If I do, I hope it's for stuff like this. But knowing me, it'll be a weird combination."

"Like matzo balls dipped in chocolate or something?"

Carol summoned a smile. She even laughed a little. "Gosh, I hope not."

He laughed, too. "I should warn my chef, just in case."

She turned serious. "Why would your chef be making the food I crave?"

Jake went somber. "Because I was thinking that you could move in with me for a while. That's what I wanted to talk to you about. There's plenty of room. You can have one of the guest wings all to yourself."

Moving into his mansion was the last thing she'd expected him to suggest. "How long is a while?"

"I don't know. Maybe five or six months. That'll give us time to shop for a house where you and the baby can live later on, and it'll give me the opportunity to be part of the pregnancy while you're staying at my place."

"But won't that cramp your style, with me waddling around your big, glitzy bachelor pad in maternity dresses?"

"You make it sound like I live at the Playboy Mansion." He made a tight face. "Or something equivalent to it."

"It's pretty darn close."

"It is not. And even if it was, I'm going to have to clean up my act when the kid is around."

"I know, but the baby isn't even born yet."

"You're twisting this all up, Carol."

Because she was afraid of moving in with him, of letting herself get that close. "I don't see why I can't stay at my apartment."

"I already told you why. I want to be part of the pregnancy. I want to get comfortable with it. And quite frankly, it bothers me to think of you being alone in the apartment. What if something happens?"

"Everything will be fine."

"But what if it isn't? We both know that bad things can happen. At least if you're staying with me, I can keep an eye on you. In fact, maybe you should just live at my house until the baby is born. That would be safer."

He sounded wonderfully protective, like the kind of man she'd always wanted to have children with. Except for him being a wild-spirited billionaire, she reminded herself.

Could he really clean up his act? Or would he succumb to his old ways, even with her living there?

"I don't know, Jake." She just couldn't fathom it. "I agree that becoming a parent is something you'll have to get used to. But me being at your house until the baby is born? That isn't necessary." She tried to make him see things a little more clearly, to recognize the problems that could arise. "Having me around 24/7 might make you feel trapped." She tore at her napkin, shredding the sides of it.

He watched her. "Looks to me like you're the one feeling trapped."

Yes, but she was also the one who might get attached, who might long for more than he was able to give. "I just don't want to jump the gun."

"Come on, give it a try. Let me keep you safe." He motioned to her still-flat stomach. "You've got my blood in you now."

His blood. His life force. "I couldn't handle you dating anyone while I was living there." She pushed it a step further, being as brutally honest as she could. "Or bringing women home to your bed."

"Is that what you think I'd do? With everything that's going on, that's the last thing on my mind." He crinkled his forehead. "Are you going to go back to online dating?"

"Now?" How could he even ask her such a ridiculous question? "Of course not. I'm having a baby."

He stared her down. "So am I."

"But you're not the one who's pregnant."

"So just imagine that I am."

She almost laughed at the image he presented. Yet she was touched by his daddy-like determination, too. Heaven help her, but she wanted him to keep her and their child safe, to be warm and attentive.

"Okay, then, we'll try it," she said, warning her fluttery heart to be still. "But if it gets too complicated, I need the option of moving out before the baby comes."

"Deal." He softened his voice. The look in his eyes gentled, too. "Only, it's already complicated, Carol."

"I know." But with how romantic he was making her feel, she was concerned that it could get much, much worse.

Carol should have listened to Jake and allowed him to hire the movers to pack for her. But she'd insisted that she was perfectly capable of boxing up her own belongings.

Of course Jake had offered to help, and he'd been watching her like a hawk, squawking every time he thought she was lifting something too heavy. She'd packed everything extralight, but that wasn't the problem. Carol was battling waves of nausea, and she didn't want Jake to know.

She glanced across the kitchen at him. He was wrapping glassware in paper, just as she was.

He looked up at her and frowned. "Are you all right?"

"I'm fine," she lied.

"You're as white as a sheet."

"I'm okay."

"Then why do you look like you're about to topple over?" He abandoned the glassware and came over to her. "You need to get off your feet."

"Maybe for a few minutes." She let him escort her to the couch, where she sat down and admitted the truth. "I'm dizzy, but I've got morning sickness, too."

He looked confused. "But it's afternoon."

"It can happen at any hour. The queasiness just started, about ten minutes ago. For the very first time."

"Damn. Do you want a cup of water or anything?"

"Soda sounds good." Hopefully it would settle her stomach. "There's lemon-lime pop in the fridge."

He headed to the kitchen, returning with the drink she'd requested. Carol gripped the can, appreciating how cold it was. She flipped the top and took a small sip.

"Thank you," she said after she swallowed it.

"You're welcome, but you still look like hell."

"Gee, thanks."

He sat beside her. "I didn't mean it like that."

She sipped a bit more of the soda, afraid she might faint, falling headfirst onto his lap. "If I pass out, don't panic."

"Oh, crap. Really? Tell me what to do."

She didn't have a clue. She'd never lost consciousness before. "Nothing."

"Nothing?" He sounded on the verge of panic already. "Maybe you should put your head between your knees. I always heard that's what someone should do. But maybe not in your condition." Clearly, he was clueless, too. "Do you want to lie down?"

"Yes, I think I should." She handed him the soda, and he moved off the couch, giving her room to stretch out. Between the wooziness and the nausea, she wasn't doing well.

Carol reclined, and Jake towered over her, peering down at her face. This had to be miserable for him.

"I'm sorry," she said.

"It's not your fault." He blew out a ragged breath. "I can finish packing. There isn't that much left to do."

"You're so helpful." She teased him, trying to ease the tension. "Are you going to change diapers when the baby is born, too?"

"I guess I'm going to have to learn. But I also think I should hire a nanny to go back and forth between your place and mine. I can turn the second guest wing in my house into the nanny's quarters. Then she can stay there whenever the baby sleeps at my place."

As opposed to him coming over to Carol's house to

tuck their child in at night, like he'd originally planned? "I just wish that feeling lousy wasn't part of this. Being queasy is the worst."

"I hope I don't get queasy when I have to change a dirty diaper. I used to gag when I was kid and I had to pick up dog poop."

She squinted up at him. This was a weird conversation, but at least it was helping her focus on something besides being sick. "You had a dog?"

"No. But my sisters and I used to pet-sit for a neighbor. I was terrible at it. I wonder if we should get our kid a puppy, though."

"That's sweet. But maybe we'll stick to stuffed animals at first." She sat up and reached for the soda, taking it from him. "I'm starting to feel better now."

His gaze locked on to hers. "Are you sure?"

"Yes." She brought the can to her lips. But a second later, the queasiness came back tenfold.

When her stomach roiled, she knew she was going to throw up. She just hoped that she made it to the bathroom in time. Leaping forward, she thrust the soda at him, but he wasn't expecting it, and the drink fell between them and spilled to the floor. That didn't stop Carol from dashing off down the hall.

Thank goodness she managed to get to the bathroom in time to empty the contents of her stomach into the toilet.

Afterward, she flushed the handle. On wobbly legs, she stood and rinsed her mouth, then turned around and realized that she'd left the door open. And much to her mortification, Jake was standing there. Had he been there the whole time?

"Let me help," he said as he removed a washcloth from the towel rack and ran it under the tap.

He handed her the cool cloth so she could dampen her skin. She thanked him and sank back to the floor, sitting beside the commode. He got onto the floor with her.

"I feel like I have a hangover," she said.

He smiled. "I'll bet you've never been *that* drunk in your life."

"That's true. But it's what I imagine it must feel like." Less embarrassed, she was glad he was here. "I'll bet you've been *that* drunk."

"Hell, yes. I've prayed to the porcelain more times than you ever will."

"I just might beat your record if this keeps up." She lifted the washcloth from her forehead and set it on her lap. "But I'm all right now."

"You said that right before you ran in here."

"I know, but I mean it this time. I'm actually getting kind of hungry."

"Really?" He seemed relieved. "For what?"

A treat instantly came to mind. "A steamed artichoke. Doesn't that sound good?"

"Not particularly." He gave her a perplexed look. "Who wants an artichoke after they throw up?"

She did apparently. And they'd never even been her favorite food. She liked them, sure. But they sounded heavenly right now. "Will you go the store and get me one? Actually, you better make it two, in case one isn't enough."

He looked dumbfounded. "Do they sell them already steamed?"

"Of course not. I'll have to cook them. Go on." She pushed at his shoulder. "You can go to the farmer's market down the street. They'll be fresher there."

"Oh, wow," he said. "This is a craving, isn't it?" His dark eyes lit up. "You're having your first craving."

"I guess I am." And it was mighty powerful, too. But she was going to think of it as her second craving. Because the first one was for Jake himself on those forbidden nights that she'd climbed into bed with him.

Like a dutiful father-to-be, he left to get the artichokes, mumbling about how clever their kid was, already figuring out ways to control them.

While he was gone, she went into the living room to wipe up the spilled soda, with their brilliant little baby in tow.

Eleven

Carol had been living at Jake's house for three weeks. She still was queasy, on and off, but none of the morning sickness medications worked, so she handled it the old-fashioned way, keeping crackers in her desk at work. At home, she relaxed as much as she could.

The guest wing that had become her temporary residence was as big as her apartment, if not a little bigger. Bright and beautiful, with modern furnishings, it offered all sorts of luxuries, including a private patio surrounded by natural landscape.

Since her quarters also had a kitchen, she was able to cook for herself. She was still eating the devil out of steamed artichokes, along with whatever else she was in the mood for. The chef made special things for her, too, in the main kitchen, spoiling her with his culinary genius. His name was Raymond, and he was a charmingly robust man, old enough to be her grandfather.

Raymond didn't live at the mansion. He came and went, providing meals, per Jake's request. Typically, Jake fixed his own breakfast, which consisted of a protein shake his trainer had designed for him. He only ate bacon and eggs and things like that when he traveled. Otherwise, he stuck to his regular routine. Carol wouldn't drink one of those awful-looking shakes if you paid her.

As for Jake's maid, she didn't live on the property, either. She arrived every Monday, like clockwork, and cleaned his private suite. Another set of housekeepers were scheduled on Mondays, too; they tidied up the rest of the mansion. Carol never left a mess for them in her wing. She'd already gotten into the habit of cleaning on Sundays before they came.

On this quiet day off, she didn't know what to do with herself. At noon, she was wandering around her wing, still dressed in her pajamas.

She didn't have any sewing left to do. Last week she'd completed the Caribbean quilt for Jake, and he'd been thrilled to receive it. He'd draped it on the wall in the room that was going to be the nursery. He thought the quilt was even more special since their child had been conceived that weekend. For a man who'd never wanted children, he was doing what he could to embrace fatherhood.

Suddenly, her phone beeped, signaling a text. When

she saw it was from Jake, her heart skipped a girlish beat.

The message read, Garrett wants to stop by and bring you something. Is that all right?

Yes. Of course, she replied.

Come to the living room and we'll wait for him.

She typed out, Be there in a few.

He ended the conversation with a simple, OK.

Carol set down her phone and went to her closet, removing a casual sundress to wear. Living in a house this big was crazy. And so was her emotional attraction to Jake. She'd been having way too many dreamy thoughts about him, and his tenderness over the baby was compounding her feelings.

But Jake was still wild at heart. She could see it every time she looked into his eyes. Becoming a parent wasn't curbing his restless spirit. If anything, the responsibility that had been thrust upon him was intensifying it.

Carol headed to the living room and spotted Jake standing at a big picture window, gazing out at the view.

She didn't disturb him or alert him that she was there. Instead, she took the time to study him: the familiarity of his body, the width of his shoulders, the way his T-shirt stretched across the muscles in his back, his long denim-clad legs.

A moment later, his posture changed, as if he'd just

sensed her presence. He turned around, and she braced herself for the impact he was sure to cause.

"There you are," he said.

"Yes." There she was, struggling with her attraction to him.

"How's Artichoke?" he asked.

Carol smiled. That had become his nickname for the baby. "Fine. It's behaving."

"So you're doing okay today, too?"

She nodded. As well as an uncomfortably smitten woman could be.

Jake remained near the window. Since she'd moved into his mansion, they'd been keeping a deliberate physical distance from each other. It didn't diminish the electricity in the air. Their chemistry buzzed like honeybees pumped up on nectar. Carol could almost taste the sexy sweetness.

Before things got too quiet, she asked, "When will Garrett be here?"

"Soon." He finally took a step forward.

But not close enough to make a difference, she thought. "Did Garrett say what he's bringing me?"

"No, but it's not from him. It's from his mom. He told her about us, so the gift probably has something to do with the baby. She would have come with him, but she isn't feeling well today."

Although Carol had met Shirley Snow a few times over the years, she didn't really know her very well. "I'm sorry to hear that."

"She's always had her ups and downs."

Carol nodded. She was aware of the older woman's health issues and how her symptoms were worse at times than others. "It was nice of her to think of me."

"Yeah, she's a sweet lady. She's got Garrett twisted up about the girl who embezzled from us, though."

Jake explained what was going on, filling Carol in about Meagan needing a job in order to get paroled. Since the crime had been committed before Carol had worked for Jake, she barely knew anything about it. When he brought up the part about Meagan having a daughter, Carol thought about the child in her own womb.

She said, "I wonder if she would have stolen the money and taken the chance of going to prison if she'd known ahead of time that she was pregnant."

"I doubt she would have risked it." He hesitated. "But it's tough to know for sure. I keep trying to give her the benefit of the doubt because of the things I did when I was young."

"It's terrible that her daughter was born under those circumstances."

"It bothers me, too, especially now that we're having a kid." Jake lowered his gaze to her stomach. "Would it be all right if I put my hand there? Just to see if it feels different from before?"

Carol didn't know what to say. If he touched her, she feared that she might like it, far more than she should. "It's too early. I'm not even showing yet."

"I know, but the baby is still in there. Of course I won't do it if you don't want me to."

"No, it's okay. You can," she offered foolishly. Refusing didn't seem like an option.

He walked up to her and placed his palm against the waist of her dress. His touch was warm and tender, affecting her in a dreamy way. She could have been floating, like their mermaid, out to sea.

But all too soon, the memory of making love with him hit her like a heap of crumbled sand. If he stripped her naked, here and now, would she fall willingly at his feet?

He kept his hand painstakingly still. But when she looked up at him and their gazes met, he wrapped his arms around her, pulling her toward him.

They stared at each other, poised for a kiss.

The doorbell rang, jarring both of them to their senses. Jake jumped back, and Carol smoothed her dress.

"Ready?" he asked.

She nodded and followed him to the front door to greet their guest. Garrett came inside, but he told them that he couldn't stay long, so they stood in the foyer, dwarfed by its museum-height ceiling and stylish staircase.

Garrett was dressed in business attire, as if he'd just come from the hotel. He was as polished as ever, with his slicked-back hair and impeccable posture. He was holding Carol's gift, wrapped in plain white tissue paper.

"Hey there," he said to her.

"Hey yourself." She'd always liked him. But they

had similar personalities, with practical natures. Of course, the exception was when Carol had gone wild on that weekend with Jake, playing around and getting pregnant.

As the father of her child stepped back, Garrett handed Carol the package. Even before she opened it, he said, "It's a medicine bag that my mom made for you. She gave one to Jake when he was younger, and to Max, too. And me, of course. And now that you're becoming part of our little ragtag group, she wanted you to have one, as well."

Carol nearly cried on the spot. She wanted to belong to them. She removed the tissue paper and unveiled the leather bag. It was exquisitely beaded, from top to bottom.

"It's beautiful," she said, her voice catching. "So incredibly beautiful. Please thank your mother for me, and tell her that I'll come see her when she's well enough for company."

"She'd like that." Garrett gestured to the bag. "It's bigger than the one Mom gave us guys, but she made it so you could include things for the baby, too. In fact, she already put some stones inside of it to get you started."

"Really?" Carol lifted the flap and peered into the bag. Sure enough, she saw pretty little rocks.

"They're easy to identify," Garrett said. "I can tell you what's there and what they mean."

"Okay, then tell me." She desperately wanted to know.

"All right. The red one promotes fetal growth, the

green one aids child development and the pink one stimulates a bonding between an infant and its mother."

She loved the sentiment already. "What are the names of each of those stones?"

"Red jasper, green aventurine and pink calcite."

"That is easy." She noticed a multicolored crystal stone that he hadn't mentioned. "What about this last one?"

"That's angel aura quartz. Jake told me that he was concerned about keeping you and the baby safe, and when I mentioned that to Mom, she thought it would help. To bring angels to you."

Feeling far too emotional, Carol glanced at Jake. He was looking at her in the same way, as if both of their hearts had just gotten stuck in their throats.

After she and Jake broke eye contact, Garrett said, "You can put anything in the bag that feels special to you. There are no rules about what goes inside."

"It's a perfect gift," she replied. "I'm going to hang it beside my bed."

"I'm glad you like it." Garrett straightened his tie out of what seemed like habit. "But I better head out now. I've got a meeting."

"Thank you again. And please give your mom a hug from us."

The hotel magnate smiled, his rugged features softening. "From you and the baby?"

"Yes." She returned his smile. She and the little one in her womb were a package deal.

Garrett turned to Jake and said goodbye to him, too.

Jake clapped him on the back, and they embraced, both of them appearing strong and brotherly.

Once they separated, Garrett exited the mansion, leaving Jake and Carol alone.

After Garrett was gone, Jake and Carol remained in the foyer. He couldn't stop looking at her, no matter how hard he tried. He was mesmerized by how reverently she was handling the medicine bag. Everything about her drew his attention.

"You were right about that being the perfect gift," he said.

"I'll have to think about what I'm going to put in it. But I love how Shirley included the stones already."

"It's interesting that you're going to keep it beside your bed. That's where I keep mine."

"You do? I never noticed yours there." She quickly amended, "But I haven't spent time in your suite."

And especially not in the vicinity of his bed, he thought. "It's hanging with a dream catcher Shirley also made for me."

"I always wondered about those, with the netting and the feathers and how popular they've become."

"They're supposed to protect you while you're sleeping. The bad dreams get caught in the net and break apart by morning. But the good ones slip through the hole in the center and glide down to the feathers, allowing you to keep those dreams."

She met his gaze. "Do you have bad dreams, Jake?"

"I used to, after I lost my family. I dreamed about the

crash. And the fire. I would see the car burning in my nightmares, with demons rising up out of the ashes." He glanced at his arm, where the image of the fire god was. Uncta was his first tattoo. He'd had to wait until he'd turned eighteen to get it. His ink had been a long time coming.

She shifted her feet. "I had bad dreams when I first lost my family, too. But I can't recall them now. Not the details, anyway. But I do remember that I used to wake up crying in the middle of the night." She pressed the medicine bag closer to her body. "Then I would be afraid to go back to sleep."

"That's understandable." He thought about how her family had died, asleep in their beds, poisoned by a deadly gas while she was at a slumber party. "What happened that morning, Carol? Who found them?" This wasn't a conversation he'd intended to have. But for whatever reason, he needed to know. "It wasn't you, was it?"

"No." She tightened her hold on the bag. "But it became apparent, rather quickly, that something was wrong. My mom was supposed to come get me that morning and take me home. It was only a few blocks from our house, but Mom didn't want me coming back by myself. Of course she never showed up. She didn't answer the phone when I called, either, so my friend's mother drove me home."

"The mom who was hosting the slumber party?"

"Yes. Mrs. Reynolds. Later, I found out that her first name was Nancy. Anyway, when we got there, the front door was locked, but our garage had a little window. Nancy peered into it and saw that both cars were there."

"You didn't have a key?"

She shook her head. "My parents didn't allow us kids to be home by ourselves so there was no reason for me to have a key. They were waiting until I was a little older to give me that kind of responsibility. They were overprotective. It's just who they were." She paused, took a breath. "Nancy brought me back to her house and called the police. They're the ones who found my family."

And everything changed for her, Jake thought. Just the way it had changed for him. "I'm probably going to be overly protective with our child." He was already having concerns about keeping the baby safe in Carol's womb.

"I understand how you feel, after everything we've both been through. What happened to us shaped who we are."

"They say that time heals all wounds. But that's a false statement. The wound is still there, maybe not as fresh, but it's still there."

After a second of silence, she asked, "Was there a service for your family?"

"No. There was nothing. My grandfather said he couldn't afford to pay for it. And my aunt certainly couldn't, not with how broke she was. So I just said some prayers for them in my mind. What about yours?"

"My parents had a burial plan, so it was prepaid. But my sisters weren't included in the plan. They hadn't bought plots for us kids. No one thinks their kids are going to die. Our church took up a collection, so my sisters could be buried with my parents."

"What was it like for you, attending the service?" In some ways, Jake was glad that he didn't have to stand at a grave site, looking like the broken orphan that he was.

"It was surreal. Like a bad dream. Except that when you wake up, you know it's real."

His heart hurt for her, and for himself, too. "Maybe I'll ask Shirley to make our baby a couple of dream catchers." He wanted their son or daughter to dream well. "One for the nursery here and one for the nursery at your place, after we get you settled into your new home."

She smiled. "That's nice, Jake. Maybe she can attach some of the angel crystals to them. For extra protection."

"I like that idea." He liked her being at his house, too, even if it was far more intense than it should be. "You were right. It was too early for me to feel the baby inside you." All he'd felt was his hunger for her and the kiss it had almost triggered. "But that should get easier when your tummy gets bigger."

"Hopefully it will, especially if the baby is moving around." She lowered her voice. "Otherwise, it just seems like you and me doing something we shouldn't be doing."

"It was my fault for pulling you toward me. I shouldn't have done that. In the future, I'll be careful not to do anything to stir those types of feelings again."

"I appreciate that. But I'm going to go and hang this up." She lifted the medicine bag. "So I'll see you later."

"Sure. See you." He assumed that hanging up the medicine bag was just an excuse to get away from him and the emotion it caused. But he let her go. He couldn't keep her in his clutches, not when he'd just promised to be careful. Even if, in spite of it all, he still wanted to kiss her something fierce.

Twelve

As Carol's pregnancy progressed, so did her friendship with Garrett's mother. Over the past few months, they'd formed a nice bond, spending time together whenever it was possible. Today Shirley had invited her over for a cup of tea.

While they sipped spiced chai and chatted, Carol spotted a delicately painted statuette that she hadn't noticed before. "You got a unicorn."

"I found it online. You know me. I like to collect magical things, even if it's just a mishmash of stuff. When Garrett first bought this resort, he offered to build me a house on the property, like he did for himself, but I enjoy living at the hotel."

Carol nodded. Shirley resided in one of the penthouses, with a spectacular view of the beach.

"I like knowing that there's activity around me, and when I'm feeling well enough to get out, all I have to do is go down to the lobby. I can dine in the restaurant of my choice and get my hair and nails done in the salon. Sometimes I even hang out with the concierge and talk to the guests."

"Hotel living at its finest."

"Indeed, it is. I used to be a hotel maid. That's what I did when Garrett was growing up. Of course I was sick a lot and kept losing jobs. But he grew up in this type of environment."

"I didn't know that." But it made sense that Garrett had become an hotelier.

"I'm blessed now. My son's success has spoiled me."

"You must be really proud of him."

Shirley sighed. "I am, more than I can say. He provides everything I need—the best food, the best medical care, everything I didn't have before. I probably wouldn't be alive today if it wasn't for him."

Carol studied her companion. She appeared older than her fifty years, but she was still pretty, with graying black hair, strong-boned features and deep brown eyes. Carol's mother would have turned fifty-three this year, if she'd lived.

"What's wrong?" Shirley asked. "Did I say something that made you feel sad?"

"No. I was just thinking about my mom."

"Oh, I'm sorry. I can only imagine how much you

miss her. I'll bet if she was here, she would be thrilled about the baby. Look how cute that little bump of yours is."

Feeling better already, Carol glanced down at her tummy. "It is, isn't it?" Jake certainly thought so. He was always eager to touch it, even if their attraction still sparked like a lightning rod between them. Somehow, though, she managed to get through those heartskittering moments, difficult as they were. "Odd as it sounds, I actually like being pregnant."

"There's nothing odd about that. You're glowing, like an expectant mother should be."

"I'm at eighteen weeks already. Oh, and tomorrow is our second ultrasound, the midpregnancy one, where we might be able to find out if it's a boy or a girl. The first one was too early to tell."

Shirley clapped her hands together. "That is exciting. Do you have an intuition about what it might be?"

"No. But Jake and I both decided that we want to know. He's certainly been anxious about everything associated with having a baby. Sometimes he can barely sit still. He's been going to the track a lot lately, racing those cars of his."

"He's always been like that. Running with the wind. When they were boys, I used to worry about his influence on Garrett and Max. That he would pull them into trouble, too. But he never did. I think in some ways, Jake is the gentlest of all of them, even with how rebellious he is. At one time he had a healthy, happy family. He knows what stability is. He understands it."

"He's going to be a wonderful father." Carol appreciated how attentive he was to her pregnancy. "He adores the baby already."

"That must make you happy."

"Yes, of course." But it also intensified her feelings for him, the attachment she'd been battling. Being alone at night was the worst. She longed to sleep beside Jake so he could hold her. Yet if she shared his bed, she wouldn't be able to resist him. She desired him in other ways, too.

"Have you started looking at homes?" Shirley asked.

"For my permanent residence? Not yet. We will once the time gets closer. I'm just surprised we've been able to live in the same house for this long. But it's almost like having separate places, with how big the mansion is."

"Jake likes to do things on a grand scale. I'm surprised he doesn't have the nursery all ready to go."

"He's waiting to find out what we're having. Then he plans to bring his decorator in to get started."

"Be sure to let me know how the ultrasound goes." Shirley reached over to pat her arm. "Your parents would be proud of you, Carol. You're a good girl."

A good girl having a baby with a notoriously bad boy. "I'm trying to stay true to myself." Just as Jake was being true to himself, as much as either of them could in the situation they were in.

"That's all a person can do. Oh, I forgot to tell you. The job thing is finally in the works."

"You mean with Garrett and Meagan?" The last

Carol heard, Garrett was still dragging his feet, trying to decide what to do. "He went through with it?"

Shirley nodded. "He offered her a position as a stable hand, maintaining and cleaning the stables. He submitted it in writing."

"Did she accept it?"

"Yes. She responded to his note and thanked him. But they haven't seen each other in person or spoken on the phone about it. Garrett doesn't want to have any further contact with her. He wants to wait to see if the parole board approves the offer and releases her."

"Do you think they will?"

"I don't see why not. From my understanding, she's been a model prisoner."

Carol couldn't imagine being in Meagan's predicament, but she wouldn't have gotten herself into that kind of trouble in the first place, either. "I wonder if it will be awkward having Garrett as her boss."

Shirley sipped her tea. "She won't be working directly for him. Her boss will be the man who manages the barn. Garrett does spend a lot of time at the stables, though. He keeps his own horses there and rides as often as he can."

Curious, Carol asked, "What made him choose that position for her?"

"She comes from an equestrian family. Both of her brothers are in the horse industry." Shirley paused. "I know it seems strange that I got my son involved in this, but I think it will help him get over it. He was insanely angry when he first found out. Ragingly mad. I've never seen him like that before."

"Jake told me that Garrett took it personally."

"A bit too personally, if you ask me. And that's why I think it needs to get resolved."

"Why do you think it affected him so badly?"

"He won't talk about it. But I have my theories. I think he might've befriended Meagan before it happened, and what she did blindsided him. Garrett has been hurt by people he trusted before. But whatever it was with Meagan, I don't want him carrying that kind of bitterness around in his heart."

Carol glanced at the unicorn. It was surrounded by fairies and gnomes and dragons. There were mermaids in the mix, too. "I agree. It needs to get resolved."

"Meagan apologized at the sentencing, but I don't think Garrett believed that she was sorry. I did, though. I went with him just to see what sort of person this young woman was, and she seemed terribly fragile to me."

"Is that part of why you took an interest in her when her parole came up?"

"Yes, and then when I learned that she'd had a baby in prison and the child's father abandoned her before it was even born, I empathized with her even more. Garrett's daddy walked out on me when I was pregnant, so I know what that feels like. But the clincher was when I discovered that I was once acquainted with Meagan's mother. That seemed like a message from above."

"All of that makes sense to me. To Jake, too. He and I both feel bad about Meagan giving birth like that."

"And now you're well on your way to becoming parents yourselves."

"We definitely are." And tomorrow, they would be one step closer to knowing more about the ever-growing child in Carol's womb.

They were having a girl, Jake marveled, a wondrous little being with a strong and steady heartbeat. He'd attended the ultrasound with Carol. He'd sat beside her earlier that day and watched the technician slide the transducer over the gel on her stomach. He'd watched the monitor. He'd seen their daughter.

They'd been given pictures and a video of her, too. It was the most thrilling day of Jake's life, even more exciting than the first ultrasound. Last time, their unborn child had looked like an itty-bitty alien. This time, he could totally tell it was a baby. He'd already watched the video a zillion times, studying every detail, imagining how it was going to feel to hold their newborn in his arms.

"What an amazing experience," he said to Carol. He sat across from her in a patio chair beside his pool, moonlight reflecting off the water.

"I know," she replied, cradling her stomach. "It was wonderful."

He never wanted it to end. But he knew Carol would probably be headed to bed soon. Jake had no idea how he was going to sleep. He was far too wired.

"We should start coming up with names," he said. "Making a list of ones we both like."

"Sure, we can do that." She smiled at him. "You look crazy excited."

"I am. Just think of what a miracle this is. You and me. Two orphaned people, creating a little person like that. I mean, really, how beautiful is our daughter?"

Her smile turned even brighter. "She's perfect."

"I know, right?" He gazed at the mother of his child, thinking how enchanting she looked, with her hair stirring in the evening breeze, her tummy swollen from the seed he'd planted. "I can't wait for the next ultrasound, so we can see her again."

"Maybe we can give her a name that represents both of our families. You can come up with a Choctaw name, and I'll work on some Irish names."

"You're Irish?" After all of this time, how did he not know that about her?

She nodded. "From my mother's side. Both of my maternal great-grandparents were originally from Ireland."

"Whereabouts?"

"A place in East Cork called Middleton."

Jake's pulse jumped. "That's where your mother's ancestors are from? That's amazing."

"Why? Have you been there?"

"No. But the Irish built a monument honoring the Choctaw Nation, and that's where it's located."

She blinked at him. "Are you sure you're not mixing it up with something else?"

"No, I'm positive. During the Great Famine, the Choctaw Nation donated money to Ireland. Their gift was especially generous, because the Choctaw were still having struggles of their own. Prior to that, they walked the Trail of Tears, where most of them were forced to leave their ancestral homelands in what's now the southeastern US and relocate to Oklahoma. There were other tribes forced to make the journey, too, but the Choctaw were the first, with many of them dying along the way."

She seemed riveted by his story, by the past that bound his ancestors to hers. "So, later, when the Choctaw heard about how many people were dying in Ireland from the potato famine, they sent them money?"

"Yes, that's exactly it. And since then, there's been a kinship between the two. The monument is called *Kindred Spirits.* I'm not sure why they chose to put it in Middleton, though. It might have something to do with the artist."

"What does it look like?" she asked.

"It's a huge sculpture, with nine steel eagle feathers arranged in the shape of an empty bowl. The bowl represents the Great Famine, and the feathers are symbolic of the Choctaw. I've seen pictures of it online, but I'd love to see it in person sometime."

"Me, too." She cradled her stomach even more closely. "What a beautiful legacy this is for our daughter."

"We'll take her there, for sure. To visit the monument, but also to learn about the town where your mother's family was from. It will be a trip all of us can take together."

As soon as the word *together* was out of his mouth, a sense of fear punched his gut. Not at the prospect of traveling together, but at the future that would also separate them.

What was going to happen as time marched on, when Carol and their child were living in a different house from Jake? When both he and Carol started dating other people again?

He considered the possibility of Carol finding the husband she always wanted, a man who would become a stepfather to Jake's daughter. Just thinking about it twisted him up inside. The baby in Carol's womb belonged to him, not to an outsider honing in on Jake's territory.

Should he offer to marry Carol, securing his place in her life? Clearly, it would be the right thing to do. And the fear of another man taking his place was far worse than Jake buckling down and making a commitment to Carol.

Wasn't it?

Yes, he told himself. He didn't want Carol going off with someone else, no matter how scary the prospect of marrying her was to him.

"I'm getting sleepy," she said, jarring him back to the moment.

He looked into her eyes, this woman he was considering as his wife. By now, his heart was thudding in his ears. "I figured you'd want to turn in early."

She stood and smoothed her blouse over her tummy. "I'll see you in the morning."

He came to his feet, too. "I can walk you to your wing."

"That's all right. I can manage."

"I know, but I want to."

"Really, it's okay."

"Can I at least say good-night to the baby?"

"Of course." She invited him to come closer.

Immersed in myriad emotions, he put his hand on her stomach, spreading his fingers across the tiny bump that was their child. Then he glanced up and said, "Sleep well," to Carol.

"I will. It's been a nice day, but a long one, too."

She ended the connection, and he watched her walk away, the night embracing her just before she disappeared into the house.

Jake remained by the pool with a life-altering decision on his mind.

Carol got ready for the office, expecting to carpool with Jake. They rode together when their schedules meshed, and today was one of those days. But when she went into the main kitchen to meet up with him, she saw that he hadn't gotten suited up for work yet. He was a wearing a T-shirt and sweat shorts.

"Are you going in late?" she asked.

He shook his head. "I'm not going in at all. I've got too much going on in my head."

"Did something happen? Is something wrong?" Now

that she took a closer look at him, she noticed how frazzled he seemed, as if he'd been up all night. He hadn't even had his breakfast yet. His protein shake was still in the blender.

Everything else was in order, though. His state-of-the-art kitchen gleamed, the stainless-steel appliances shining like mirrors. Of course, the cleaning crew was just there yesterday.

"What's going on, Jake?"

He pulled a hand through his hair. "I think you and I should get married."

Oh, my God. Carol felt as if the refrigerator had just opened up and sucked her inside, closing off the air to her lungs.

"What do you think?" he asked.

Needing to get off her feet, she sat on a bar stool at the center island counter. "Did you say married?" She repeated his strange proposal, making sure she'd heard him correctly.

"Yeah, you know…" He made walking motions with his fingers, using both hands, mimicking a couple going down the aisle.

Carol couldn't have been more confused. "Why?" she asked. "Why do you want to get married all of a sudden?"

"For our daughter."

"That's the only reason?"

He frowned at her. "Isn't that enough?"

"No." She couldn't pretend that it was, no matter

how badly she'd always ached to be a wife. "People who get married should be in love."

"But we love our child," he countered. "And she deserves to have both of her parents in the same house, living as a couple."

"Just being in the same house with a piece of paper between us isn't going to make us a family. You know that as much as I do. You and I were both raised by parents who loved each other, as well as their kids. That's the kind of family I want."

"But our baby girl needs us to be together."

He wasn't listening, she thought. "I'm not talking about our daughter. I'm talking about us."

"But I don't want you to marry someone else."

She blinked at him. "What?"

He poured his foamy green shake into a glass and took a swig. "If you don't marry me, then someday you'll marry some other dude and our poor kid will be shifted back and forth, between him and me."

"So that's what this is all about? You being jealous of a man who doesn't even exist yet?"

"What's so wrong with that? Me not wanting him to hone in on my child? Or my woman?"

She narrowed her eyes at him. "I'm not your woman."

"You could be, if you married me. I'd give you everything, Carol. You'd want for nothing."

"Except love?" Her heart hurt from the thought of it.

"You're not in love with me, either, so what difference does that make?"

"It matters. It's the dream I've always had."

"Of being with a guy who is nothing like me? Well, excuse me for offering to marry you and ruining your picture-perfect dream."

"That isn't fair." Even now, as she gazed into his deep dark eyes, she knew that she was capable of loving him. That maybe she was already well on her way. But God help her, she wasn't about to say it. Just thinking it could be true, just realizing that it might be happening, made her want to cry.

"Please, Carol. Say yes."

"I can't." She couldn't put herself in a position that might result in her loving a man who might never feel the same way about her. Already she could feel her soul being crushed.

He persisted. "Just think of how beautiful the wedding could be. We could get married on the beach. And we could have a big, sweeping reception and feed each other cake and do all of the things brides and grooms are supposed to do."

Damn him for making it sound so idyllic, for putting those images in her head. "Yes, the ceremony would be beautiful. But that's just a party. A fancy event." Something Jake excelled at. "It wouldn't be our day-to-day lives."

"I think having you as my wife would be sexy." He put down his drink. "I'd carry you to bed right now, if you'd let me."

She shook her head, fighting the urges rising inside

her. She couldn't let him tempt her, no matter how hot he made her feel. "It would never work."

He stared across the counter at her. "We'd be good together, Carol, and you damn well know it."

Good. Bad. Right. Wrong. They would be all of those things. But without the possibility of him loving her, she couldn't break down and marry him. "My answer is still no."

"Refuse all you want, but this isn't over yet." With a rough catch in his voice, he stuck to his misguided plan. "I'm the father of your child and come hell or high water, I'm going to be your husband, too."

Thirteen

Jake worked on Carol over the next two weeks, trying to charm her into accepting his proposal. But he struck out.

He wasn't discouraged. He was going to keep at it. In fact, he had a ring in his pocket that he hoped would eventually sway her.

This was the perfect night to present it to her, as they were going to a black-tie charity event for his foundation. Jake was already dressed in his tuxedo.

He figured that, by now, she was ready, too. He knocked on the main door to her quarters, and she answered his summons.

"I just need to put on my shoes and grab my purse," she said. "Then we can go."

"No problem. We've got time." He checked her out. She was attired in a classic black gown with a beaded neckline. Her baby bump was evident, and oh-so-sweet. He was glad there was no mistaking it. Her hair, he noticed, was swept up into an elegant twist, the strawberry blond color shimmering beneath the overhead light. "You look gorgeous," he told her.

"Thank you." She stepped into a pair of low-heeled pumps. "You're rather dapper yourself."

"Thanks. I think I look like a groom."

She didn't reply, but he suspected that his comment made an impact, just as he'd intended. No doubt, it would cross her mind throughout the night.

He said, "Before we go, there's something I want you to have." He wasn't going to waste any time in turning the ring over to her. He reached into his pocket and removed the case.

"Jake." She started to protest before he even gave it to her. Clearly, she had an inkling as to what it was, based on the box.

"Just indulge me, okay?" He flipped it open and showed it to her. The gold ring had two hands holding a heart-shaped stone, with a crown at the top. The heart itself was a flawless, six-carat, fancy vivid pink diamond. "I researched Irish rings and read about Claddagh styles, so that's what this is. I had it custom made. I discussed the specifics with the jeweler, of course, but this is the first time I've ever bought a gift on my own, where I didn't ask my stylist for help." He paused to collect his thoughts. "Claddagh rings have been around for thousands of years, but jewelry experts disagree about their exact origin, so they're shrouded in mystery, even today. According to what I uncovered, there is a right and wrong way to wear to them. There are four options—single, in a relationship, engaged and married. If you wear it on your right hand, with the crown pointing toward you it means single, away from you on that hand means you're in a relationship. If you wear it on the left hand with the crown toward you, it means engaged, away from you shows that you're married."

"Oh, my." She removed the ring from the box. "The detail is exquisite. I've never seen anything like it."

"The band is shaped like an eagle feather so that part is different from traditional Claddagh rings. I did that to represent my and our baby's Choctaw blood. I got the idea from the *Kindred Spirits* monument and the style of feathers used for that." He softly added, "I wanted this to be special between us. For now, you can wear it on your right hand with the crown toward you to show that you're single. Later, when you decide that you want to marry me, you can switch it to show that we're engaged."

She inspected the design, turning it, looking at the band from every angle. "The story behind it is fascinating."

Did that mean he was making headway? "I chose a pink diamond because they're rare. I considered a bigger diamond, but that one complements the shape and size of the ring."

"Are you kidding? It's huge already. It's absolutely breathtaking."

"When we get married, I'm going to have the same type of ring designed for myself. Men can wear them, too. But I won't put a stone in mine. It will just be made of gold."

Her voice cracked a little. "I already told you that I can't marry you, Jake."

He reiterated the point he'd made earlier. "You can wear it in the single position." He just wanted to make sure the ring was in her possession. "That's all I'm asking for now."

Her breath rushed out. "Okay. I'll accept it under those conditions." She placed it on her right hand with the crown pointing toward her. "Thank you for thinking of me and the baby. I'm touched by all of the time and care you put into it. Really, truly, it's overwhelming."

Her praise and appreciation gave him hope. "Just remember that someday you *are* going to be my wife. I can't let another man be involved in raising our child."

"Don't talk about that. Let's just go out and have a nice time."

"All right." He glanced at the glittering jewel on her finger, wishing he could hold her. And kiss her. And make her marry him. But for now, this was a start.

The casino-themed party was being held at a renovated 1930s mansion that Jake owned. Typically, he rented it out for private events, but tonight it was being used for his charity. Carol thought the place was spectacular. Mostly, though, her mind was on the ring he'd given her. The color and clarity of the diamond was stunning. The cultural history associated with the ring was beautiful, too. Problem was, the design included a heart, yet Jake's proposal didn't involve loving her. He was still making his case about not wanting her to marry someone else or separate their child from him. In that regard, nothing had changed.

Nonetheless, she'd accepted the ring. Of course, she was wearing it in a way that defined her as single.

Painfully single, she thought.

Even with how hard she'd been trying to fight her feelings, Carol couldn't deny that she'd fallen in love with Jake. And for her, it didn't get any worse than that. She'd never envisioned unrequited love as being part of her future. But what woman did? That wasn't the fairy tale of which dreams were made.

"Can I get you anything?" Jake asked as they moved deeper into the mansion.

"No, thanks. I'll grab something later." There was plenty of food and drink available; the buffet was overflowing with gourmet goodies. "You don't have to babysit me. This is your party, and you need to make the rounds."

He frowned. "I don't want to leave you unattended."

"Don't worry. I'll be fine. I might even play roulette for a while."

"Okay. But in case you need to rest, take this." He pressed a key into her hand. "It's for one of the private suites. It's the first door at the top of the stairs."

"Thank you. That's very thoughtful of you."

"I just want you to be able to get off your feet. If you'd rather go home early, you can do that, too. You can take the car, and I'll catch a ride with Garrett. Either way, I know how tired you get these days, and it's probably going to be a late night."

She opened her bag and dropped the key inside. "I'll use the room if I need to." She didn't want to leave the party without him.

He angled his head. "What do your friends think, Carol?"

She gave him a perplexed look. "About what?"

"Me wanting to marry you. You've told them, haven't you?"

"Yes. And they think I should accept your offer." She'd hoped that at least one of them would see it her way, but none of them had. "They don't understand why I would refuse to marry a rich and handsome man who also happens to be the father of my child."

His gaze locked on to hers. "So they're not buying into your love theory, either?"

"Your billionaire status cancels that out, I guess. Most people are swayed by money." And once they saw the ring, they would be even more impressed.

He shrugged. "I've gotten used to that. Besides, I'd rather have them on my side, no matter what their reasoning."

"You better get going." He was standing too close for comfort, making her feel too much. "You need to tend to your guests."

"Yeah, I suppose I do. I need to find Garrett, too. He's somewhere around here. I'll check on you later, okay? I have a key to the room as well, so I can let myself in if you're up there."

She nodded and watched him walk away. He was right about his tuxedo. It did make him look like a groom.

Carol went in the opposite direction. There were makeshift casinos on both sides of the mansion, with most of the ground floor having been converted into a gambling den.

She found a roulette table with an open spot. She played badly, but it didn't matter if she won or lost. All of this was to benefit foster kids. If anyone knew how important that was, it was her and Jake and Garrett. And Max, too, of course, but he was still traveling. He'd been informed about the baby by now, though. Jake had finally called and told him.

"Well, hello there," Carol heard a woman say from beside her. She glanced over and saw Lena Kent.

"Oh, wow," Carol responded. She hadn't crossed paths with the pop star since the private island party. Lena looked like the celebrity she was, with her platinum blond hair and feline eyes. She wore a slim gold dress, slit up the front, with a white feather boa draped around her neck.

"I heard that you're having Jake's baby, and it appears the rumors are true." Lena grinned at Carol's belly. "Is that from the Caribbean?"

"Yes. Your couples-only weekend was the culprit."

Lena struck a dramatic pose, giving her feather wrap a quick toss. "So glad I could be part of it." She was still smiling. "You better make me an honorary relative."

"Absolutely. You can be her eccentric aunt."

"Her? It's a girl? Well, that settles it. I'm going to take her shopping and spoil her with all kinds of bling. Speaking of…" Lena gestured to Carol's ring. "Check out the rock on your finger. Is it from Jake?"

"He just gave it to me tonight."

Lena grabbed her hand to get a closer look. "Damn, that's nice. It's so regal with the crown, too. Perfect for you and how classy you are."

"Thank you." Carol explained the meaning behind the ring and why she was wearing it on her right hand. "I'm just not ready to marry him."

"I can see why you have your reservations. I never pictured Jake as the marrying kind. But I think it's kind of cool that he wants to settle down and try to be a husband. I'll give him points for that." Lena straightened her boa. "By the way, I'm not with Mark anymore. We stopped seeing each other soon after my birthday."

"Oh, I'm sorry. I thought you made a great pair."

"It was fun while it lasted. But I have someone new."

"Already?"

Lena laughed. "It's been a while."

Yes, of course. Carol's pregnancy was proof of that. "Does Mark still work for you?"

"No. It got too awkward. I hired another dancer to replace him." Lena nodded toward the other side of the room. "Just to make you aware, there's a hot brunette over there who's been staring at us."

"Maybe she's a fan of yours."

"I get the feeling it's you she's been watching."

Carol glanced over her shoulder. A hot brunette indeed, all decked out in red, glitzy from head to toe. "That's Susanne Monroe. She used to go out with Jake. They broke up right before he took me to the Caribbean."

"Well, that explains it, then. Because she sure seems interested in you."

"I don't know why she would care about me and my situation with Jake. Her former husband is Kenny Monroe, the pitcher, and she only dated Jake on the rebound, when she was smarting over the divorce. She and Jake weren't even together for very long."

"Maybe so, but I saw them talking earlier."

Carol frowned, fighting a stab of jealousy. "She's a guest. He has to engage with her."

Lena sighed. "Just protect what's yours, okay?"

"He isn't mine, not in the way you mean."

"The heck he isn't. He proposed to you, didn't he? That gives you a right to keep an eye on a woman who might be trying to restake her claim."

Carol didn't want to believe that Susanne was after Jake, so as the evening progressed, she tried to shut it out of her mind. It wasn't as if Susanne had become a nuisance. In fact, she left the event early. Carol saw Susanne walk out the door with a posse of other Beverly Hills socialites. Still, Lena's concern niggled at her.

Finally, when Carol needed a break from the festivities, she went upstairs to her private room.

Later, Jake appeared, like a mirage, standing beside the bed. She had no idea how much time had passed, until he told her that the party was over. She'd only closed her eyes, intending to rest, but had fallen asleep instead.

As she gazed up at him, he reminded her of a prince, come to claim his princess, his bride. She even fantasized about him leaning over to kiss her.

She didn't say anything to him about Susanne. It seemed petty now that he was here, taking her home, this beautiful man who wanted to marry her.

While at work late Monday afternoon, Carol kept gazing at her ring, wondering how it would look on her left hand.

Should she accept Jake's proposal and create a life with him?

She couldn't deny that every moment she spent with him, every instant that he was near her, felt so good, so right.

Jake was kind and protective and attentive. Wonderfully romantic. Everything she believed a husband should be. And he was trying so hard to win her over and make her his wife. Was it possible that he was falling in love with her, too? A bit too dreamy, she studied her ring again, imagining what marrying him would be like.

A second later, Carol glanced up and saw that Kristen was poking her head in the doorway. The receptionist seemed anxious.

"What's going on?" Carol asked her.

"Can I come in and talk to you?"

"Sure." She invited the fidgety girl into her office, wondering if she was having boyfriend problems again.

Kristen entered the room and closed the door. She pulled a chair closer to Carol's desk and sat on the edge of it.

Then she said, "I know you haven't agreed to marry Jake or anything. But everyone at the office knows that he asked you. He's made that pretty clear around here."

Yes, Jake had spilled the beans, professing his intentions. "Are you here to try to talk me into marrying him? Because I've already been—"

Kristen cut her off. "I'm sorry, but that's not why I'm here. It's just the opposite. I saw him today with another woman."

Carol's heart nearly jumped out of her chest. "What?"

"I went to get some food at the taco place where a lot of us go, and when I was waiting for my take-out order, I saw Jake and one of his old girlfriends having lunch, with margaritas and everything. They looked pretty cozy to me. She was even reaching across the table to touch his hand."

Carol felt sick, a wave of nausea roiling through her body. "Was it Susanne Monroe? The baseball player's ex?"

"Yep. That's who it was, the one who used to parade around here like a Kardashian." Kristen frowned. "What made you assume it was her?"

"She was at the charity event on Saturday, and Lena told me I should be wary of her. But I brushed it off. I ignored the way Susanne had been staring at me."

"I'm so sorry, Carol. I hated to even tell you that I saw Jake with her. But I don't want to see you get hurt."

She was already hurt, torn up inside. "You were right to tell me. Did he know that you saw him?"

"No. They were in a booth and his back was to me." Kristen scooted her chair a little closer. "Do you think it's possible that I misinterpreted what was going on?"

Carol looked into the younger woman's eyes. Now she was backpedaling, after everything she'd said? "Do *you* think that's possible?"

"I don't know. I just hate to be the one to ruin things for you. And since Lena warned you first, I guess what I saw was real. It's just hard to believe that Jake would go off with another woman, not with how much he wants to marry you."

"It's hard for me to fathom, too." Especially in light of how kind and protective he'd been. "I'll get Jake's side of it, and if he has a reasonable explanation, I'll take what he says into consideration." And pray, with all of her heart, that it wasn't what it seemed.

"What if he is messing around with Susanne?"

"Then I'm going to pack my belongings and leave. There's no way I could keep staying at his house with him."

"Would you quit being his assistant, too?"

"Yes, I would stop working here." Seeing Jake every day would destroy her. She would need to separate her life from his, at least the best she could. But either way, they were still having a baby together.

"I don't think I could fill in for you, not like I did when you were sick. I'd be too mad at Jake to help him out like that."

"Don't worry, I'd find another replacement. I wouldn't expect you to pick up the pieces." Carol would have to do that all on her own.

Jake sat across from Carol in his sunken living room, with his heart sinking, too. How could everyone think so badly of him?

"I wasn't having a romantic lunch with Susanne," he said, responding to the accusation that had been thrust upon him. "And her interest in you at the party wasn't sinister. She wasn't giving you the evil eye or trying to get back together with me. She was just curious about you."

Carol didn't reply. Apparently she was waiting for him to expound further.

So he continued by saying, "When she saw you and Lena, she wanted to come over and talk to you, but then she got nervous, so she just stayed away."

Carol folded her arms across her stomach. "Why would Susanne even care about me?"

"Because when I spoke to her at the party, I told her about you and the baby, and she thought it was romantic that you tamed a guy like me. It made her want to get to know you a little better." Jake reached for the ice water in front of him and took a swig. "Susanne is mixed up about her own life. She's still not over her ex. That's why she texted me today and asked me to lunch. She wanted to talk to me about how she can win Kenny back."

Carol raised her eyebrows. "She wanted advice from you? About relationships?"

"I know. Crazy, huh? She assumed that you and I were a couple. I didn't give her all the sordid details at the party. I just told her that I was planning on marrying you. So when she invited me to lunch today, I figured that I'd set her straight about us and tell her that I wasn't qualified to help her with Kenny."

"Kristen said that Susanne was reaching across the table for your hand."

"That's true. She did that. But it was only after I admitted that you've been refusing to marry me."

Carol unfolded her arms. "I'm sorry, Jake, that everyone jumped to conclusions."

"So you believe me?"

"Yes, I do. And I'm sorry that Susanne is still hurting over Kenny. But we aren't the role models for her happiness."

"I wish we were." He got up and sat beside her. "I still don't understand why you won't marry me."

"I was thinking about it, before Kristen came to my office and threw me for a loop."

"Really?" His mood brightened. "You were?"

"Yes, but I was thinking about love, too."

Damn. Did that she mean was still going to hold out for another guy? "What if you never find the love of your life? Or what if you think you found him and he turns out to be a jerk. Will you marry me then? Or am I never going to measure up to your dream?"

"Oh, Jake." She sighed. "If only you knew."

Now he was really confused. "If I only knew what?"

Her voice jittered. "That I already met the man I love. That he's already part of my life."

Suddenly he felt as though the world was caving in on him. "There's someone else? How is that even possible? The only person you've been spending time with is me."

She just stared at him. *Really* stared at him.

Holy hell. Realization dawned in his stupid male brain. "So it's me?" He even tapped his chest, identifying himself. "I'm the one?"

She nodded briskly, shakily.

"You actually love me? Like *love* me, *love* me?"

"Yes," she replied, leaning closer to him.

This should have been good news. He should have rejoiced in her admission. But Jake panicked instead. He didn't know anything about that kind of love. He'd done everything in his power to avoid those types of feelings.

He stood and moved toward the window. And as soon he turned back around, facing Carol once again, he panicked even more. Her eyes were filled with pain.

"I'm sorry," he said. "I wasn't expecting…"

"I have to go," she said. "I have to pack."

"You're leaving? What? No." His freak-out was getting worse. "Stay and we'll figure this out."

"There's nothing to figure. I can't live here anymore. I can't handle this."

He wasn't handling it, either. But he couldn't bear to lose her. "Please, I still want to marry you. I still want to create a life for our child."

She looked at him as if he'd just lost his mind. "How can you marry me when you won't even sit next to me? What kind of example is that going to set for our daughter?"

As much as he wanted to prove that he could still be a good husband and father, he couldn't bring himself to return to her side. He was struggling to breathe, forcing air in and out of his lungs. Maybe she was right. Maybe he was losing his mind. "I just need a minute."

"Take all the time you need, but I have to get out of here."

She got up from the sofa, and when she left the room, Jake was still standing with his back to the window, his feet frozen to the floor.

Fourteen

Carol moved swiftly, getting her suitcase ready, needing to escape. She hadn't intended to tell Jake that she loved him, and now that she had, it was the worst day of her adult life.

In the middle of her packing, Jake entered the room, invading her space, torturing her heart.

"You didn't have to follow me in here," she said.

"Yes, I did. It just took me a minute to get my feet moving."

Right. The minute he'd needed to get his emotions together. Thing was, he didn't look any less stressed. Even now, he was pulling a hand through that messy hair of his. The troubled rebel, she thought. The man who'd burrowed his way into her soul.

"I wish I hadn't fallen for you," she said.

"No one has ever been in love with me before. I don't know what to do with it, Carol."

"You're supposed to accept it and return the feeling. It's funny, because when I was contemplating marrying you, I wondered if you were falling in love with me, too. But I was just being silly and dreamy." And wrong, she thought, so very wrong.

He lowered his hand from his hair. "I'd rather just keep things simple."

"And marry someone you don't love?" That was far from simple to her. "That isn't how marriage is supposed to work."

"Not traditionally, but it can be whatever people decide to make it." He shifted his stance. "And maybe in time I'll get used to…"

She studied him from beneath her lashes. "Get used to what, a one-sided relationship where I love you but you don't love me?"

"I'm just trying to hold on to what we have."

"What we have is a wreck." Carol took an audible breath, the sound engulfing the room. "I'm going to call Shirley and ask if I can stay there for a few days." She didn't want to be alone, and she knew that Garrett's mother would comfort her more than any of her other friends could. "I'm not taking everything with me today. I'll come back for the rest of my belongings, but you won't see me at the office again. I can't work for you, Jake. I'll call a temp agency and arrange for my replacement, then you can hire someone permanently when you're ready to tackle that."

He glanced at the hastily folded clothes she'd placed on the bed. "I don't want you to do this."

"I know. You still want me to marry you. Do you know how crazy that sounds?"

"I can't help it. In my mind, you're still meant to be my wife." He glanced at her stomach. "You and me and our daughter. We're supposed to be together."

She disagreed. "Not like this we aren't."

"There's nothing I can say or do to keep you here?"

"No." She couldn't force him to love her, to feel things he didn't feel. Still, he looked so lost, so confused, that she wanted to wrap her arms around him. But what good would that do? She was just as lost and confused as he was. "It's better for us to live separate lives and share custody of the baby, like we'd planned to do originally."

When she reached down to remove her ring and return it to him, he held up his hands, like a gunslinger who was about to be shot.

"Don't you dare give that back." He lifted his hands a little higher. "I refuse to take it."

"Jake, please."

"No. No way." He shook his head, as stubborn as a man could be. "Besides, what does it matter if you keep wearing it? It still says that you're single."

"It's different now." Single or not, wearing it was hurtful. The ring represented everything she loved about him. His warmth. His generosity. The kind and caring father he'd become. The *Kindred Spirits* legacy they shared.

After she removed it from her finger, she placed it in its original box. Then she put the box inside her medicine bag and packed it. With Jake's refusal to take the diamond back, it was the best she could do. Just leaving the ring behind would seem unkind, and she couldn't bear to create more pain between them.

She said, "When I thought something might be going on between you and Susanne, I was prepared to walk away. But I never thought I'd be leaving under these circumstances."

"I never imagined it ending at all." Jake cleared his throat. "On the night of the fund-raiser when I came into the room to check on you, and you opened your eyes and looked at me, it seemed like we were already married."

"I felt like a bride when I woke up and saw you. A princess, waiting for her groom. I even fantasized about you kissing me."

He stepped a little closer. "I wish I would have."

She backed away from him. "It wouldn't have mattered, not now."

He didn't move forward again or try to close the gap between them. He conceded, allowing her the distance she needed, but it didn't help ease her pain. She hurt just the same.

"I'll let you finish packing," he said. "Just let me know when you're ready to go, and I'll put your luggage in your car for you."

"Thank you." She didn't know what else to say. "It's just the one bag."

"You still shouldn't lift it."

He exited the room, and she fought the urge to cry. Carol dreaded the future, afraid that no matter how many years went by or how separate their lives became, she would never stop loving him.

Jake spent the next two days holed up in his house. His big, hollow mansion. He hadn't felt this alone since his family died. He missed Carol something awful.

He understood why she left. But he couldn't bear not having her here with him. He wanted nothing more than to make her his wife. And not just because of the baby.

It was the joy of being with Carol.

The same type of joy that had been snuffed out when his family's car had crashed and burned.

Was that the reason he'd been unable to return Carol's love? Yes, he thought, it was. Creating a family, *a true family*, like the one he'd lost was frightening to him. So he'd offered her a half-assed marriage instead.

What was he going to do about it? Sit here and wallow in his mistake, in the heartache of being an idiot? Letting Carol go made no sense, none whatsoever.

Still, he was scared. Since she'd been gone, he'd been dreaming about the crash, his childhood nightmares returning with a fiery vengeance. The dream catcher beside his bed hadn't saved him from reliving the pain. Nothing would, except facing his fears.

Determined to conquer them, Jake went out to the

garage and climbed into the SUV he'd bought to accommodate the baby. Only, his daughter wasn't arriving today. Today he was going back to his own youth, to the house where he'd grown up.

For him, that was as close as it got to his family having a grave site. If their spirits were anywhere, it would be at the home where all of them had lived.

Lived and loved, he thought.

Jake drove to the San Fernando Valley, heading toward his old neighborhood. His parents didn't own the home where they'd raised him and his siblings. It was a well-maintained rental, a house that had belonged to a corporation, much like the company Jake owned now.

Was that why he'd started buying properties? To give other people nice, safe places to live? He'd never really analyzed the emotional impact of his investments.

He turned onto his long-ago street and parked in front of the ranch-style house. It looked different yet somehow the same. The paint was changed, the windows trimmed in blue instead of red. The lawn was less green, a result, most likely, of water conservation associated with the current California drought. The tree that graced the yard was bigger, though, its branches reaching toward the sky.

When Jake was small, he used to offer to help with the yard work. Then later, it became a chore that had been expected of him. Sometimes he'd complained, but mostly he'd enjoyed spending time alone with his dad.

Reflective, Jake sat back in his seat. Since he didn't want to intrude on the new residents, he stayed in the car. He couldn't tell if they had kids. There were no outward signs of children, not like when he used to leave his bike in the walkway.

It felt good to be here, to think about the sweetness from his youth. He wanted to provide that kind of family for his daughter. He wanted it for himself and Carol, too. Being afraid to love her was wrong. He needed to give her his heart, openly, fully.

He understood his feelings now. They were so clear, so obvious. But was he ready to do this, to admit that he loved her?

Yes, he thought. He was ready, willing and able.

Should he text Carol ahead of time or just show up unannounced? He opted for the phone, giving her a chance to prepare. He typed, A lot going on. Need to talk.

After he sent the message, he waited. Then waited some more.

He tried not to panic about Carol not responding. She might not be in the vicinity of her phone. It didn't mean that she was ignoring him.

Trying to keep from going stir-crazy, he shifted his attention to the tree that had grown so big. Sometimes his sisters used to sit beneath it, surrounded by their friends, paging through fashion magazines and yapping about the styles they liked. He also remembered when a neighbor's cat had gotten caught in the tree. Nobody called the fire department the way they did on TV. Jake's bold and beautiful mother had climbed up there, via a ladder, and coaxed the cat down. The frightened little tabby went home to its owner, only to run away another time and never be seen or heard from again.

Jake frowned, disturbed that the story didn't end well. But that didn't change the purpose of coming back to his family, of seeking them out. It didn't change how he felt about Carol, either. If anything, it was a reminder that life was neither good nor bad. It was simply what you made of it, and he wanted it to be good and happy and whole.

When his phone pinged, he grappled with the device and nearly dropped it.

Carol's response was What's going on?

Sitting in front of my old house.

What old house?

From when I was a kid.

I don't understand.

Will explain in person. Things are different with me now. Can I come over?

She agreed with a simple Yes.

But that was all the encouragement Jake needed.

Grateful for a second chance, he took one final look at the house. He was wrong about his family's spirits being here. They'd moved on a long time ago. What

Jake had encountered was his own spirit, the boy he once was, growing into the man he'd become.

Carol was anxious to know what Jake meant when he'd texted that things were different now. But she was nervous about seeing him, too. Overall, she was a mess, inside and out.

Before she'd seen his text, she'd been watching TV, mindlessly, in her pajamas, without a stitch of makeup. So now, she rushed to get herself together, applying lip gloss and mascara and putting on a maternity blouse and leggings.

She hadn't told Shirley that Jake was coming over. The older woman was napping in her room.

As soon as a knock sounded on the door, Carol tried to center herself with a calming breath. But it didn't do any good. She was still nervous.

She opened the door, and there he was. The father of her child. The man she loved with every troubled, aching beat of her heart.

He looked strong and beautifully wild, much as he always did. Yet something about him *did* seem different. It was his eyes, she thought. She saw a sense of calmness beneath the wild, as if the restlessness that normally drove him was gone. So what did that mean? How did that affect what was happening between them?

Carol gestured to her surroundings. "Come in."

"Thanks."

He entered the suite, and they stood in the living room. She longed to touch him, to put her hand against his jaw and feel the slight bristle of beard stubble there, but she fussed with the hem of her blouse instead.

"Where's Shirley?" he asked.

"She's resting. Do you want to go to the guest room where I'm staying?" She didn't want to have a private discussion out in the open, in case Shirley got up.

"Sure. That would be good."

She led him down a short hallway, and they went into the colorfully decorated room and closed the door, silence streaming between them.

Then he said, "I'm sorry I hurt you, Carol."

"I'm sorry I hurt you, too." She'd never meant to cause him pain. "I still don't understand why you're here, though, and how going to your old house factors into it."

"I was searching for my family, hoping to feel their spirits and find a sense of peace. Since you left me, I've been having nightmares again, like I did after they first died."

"Did it work? Did you connect with your family?"

"No. But I connected with myself and the reason I couldn't commit fully to you. It was because I was afraid that if I loved you the way my parents loved each other, something would go wrong. But if I only went halfway, loving our child but keeping you at arm's length, everything would be okay."

Now she wanted to touch him even more. But she listened to him instead, letting him get all of his thoughts out.

He said, "After you got pregnant, and I started worrying about you finding another husband and involving him in our daughter's life, I didn't even stop to consider that I might be falling in love with you. Or that you were on the verge of falling for me." He moved closer to her. "So when you finally told me how you felt, I panicked and pushed you away. But I do love you, Carol, and I want to marry you for all the right reasons."

Tears rushed to her eyes, and she reached out to skim his jaw, allowing herself the touch she craved. Beneath her fingers, his skin was warm, his beard stubble rough. She ran her hands over his entire face, smoothing back his hair to trace his childhood scar.

"I would be honored to marry you. For all the right reasons," she added. What she'd seen in his eyes when he'd first arrived, the change in them, was love. She knew that now. "I missed wearing the ring you gave me."

"Wear it now."

"I'll wear it forever." She removed it from her medicine bag and placed it on her left hand, putting it in the engaged position and sealing their future with a diamond heart, an Irish crown and a Choctaw feather.

He leaned in to kiss her, and she reveled in the life they would be building together. Carol couldn't imagine a more beautiful moment. This was the proposal she'd always longed for—a dream come true.

Jake and Carol waited for Shirley to awaken from her nap to tell her the news. She was thrilled, of course, hugging them like there was no tomorrow.

But there would be plenty of tomorrows, Jake thought. He and Carol had the rest of their lives to be together.

He took his new fiancée back to his house, and as soon as they entered the mansion, he said, "I can sell this place and we can get something homier. Like what I was going to buy for you and the baby. Only, all of us can live there together."

She cocked her head. "Really? Are you sure you want to relocate?"

"I'd rather start fresh with a home that complements both of us. But it still needs to be big enough for more kids."

Her eyelids fluttered. They were standing in the foyer, with a chandelier shining above them. "More kids? Are you expecting the condoms to fail again?"

"No. I'm thinking we could actually plan to expand our family. We don't want Artichoke to be an only child, do we?"

"You're right." She smiled like the dickens. "We should give her some siblings."

"We can have three altogether." There had been three kids in his family, just as there had been in hers. "We'll make that our lucky number." Jake put his hand on Carol's tummy. "But first we need to bring this one safely into the world."

"We will. Our little girl is going to be just fine."

"Yes, everything will be okay." He'd found his peace, his life, his woman. "My parents would have adored you."

"Mine would have been crazy about you, too. They'd be so happy for me right now."

"When we get resettled, we can display all of our pictures, old and new." He studied her, thinking how amazing she was. "I have a bunch of photos stored away from when I was kid. But now I want to bring them out in the open."

"Pictures of my family have always given me comfort. But I've never been back to the house where they died. Maybe I should go there, like you did with your old house, just to come full circle, too." She studied him with the same kind of admiration he felt for her. "You were right when you said that I overcompensated after I lost them, that I was trying to be so good. I didn't let myself grieve the way I should have. I even felt guilty and weak when I used to cry in the middle of the night. I wanted to be stronger than that."

"You are strong. So am I. But we're stronger as a couple than we are apart." He took her in his arms. "Come lie down with me, Carol. I want to hold you."

She nuzzled against him. "I want to hold you, too."

They proceeded to his room. After removing their shoes, they climbed into bed. Sunlight streamed into the room, slipping through the blinds.

"I've missed being with you," he said.

"You're with me now, and you always will be." She leaned onto her side to face him. "I'm so happy that you love me. I feel like I'm dreaming."

"But you aren't. We're both wide-awake." He unbuttoned the first few buttons of her blouse to get a peek at her bra. He noticed that it was made of cotton and bits of lace. "Look how pretty you are." He toyed with the lace. "Pretty and pregnant."

"I like being pregnant. Shirley told me that I glow."

"You do. So do you want to get married at the beach?"

She nodded. "With you in a tuxedo and me in a long, breezy white dress. I can carry a red rose bouquet since that's the type of flower I always envisioned in my wedding."

Jake remembered her telling him that before. She'd even put a red rose pattern on the quilt she'd made herself when she was younger, with patches of material that represented her future. A future that was now coming true. "We can have the wedding at Garrett's resort. Lots of people get married there, along the shore."

Her eyes lit up. "That would be perfect. I want Shirley to be part of the ceremony. She's as close to a mother as either of us has now. Oh, and maybe we can hire Lena to perform at the reception."

Jake teased her, thinking about the party that had started it all. "Yeah, and we can have our first dance inside of a cage."

She laughed. "We can make 'Couples Only' our wedding song."

"Sure. Why not? But we need to set Lena straight about Susanne."

"Of course, and we'll clear it up with Kristen, too. You should introduce me to Susanne so we can invite her to be a guest."

"I'm sure she would be glad to attend."

"Good. I don't want there to be any bad feelings or gossip. I want our wedding to be as joyous as we feel."

"I'm going to ask both of my foster brothers to be my best men. Max will be back from his sabbatical soon, so we can set the date anytime. First, we'll have to talk to Garrett about his schedule and when he can make the resort available to us. He has an event planner on staff that can help us, too."

She untucked Jake's T-shirt from his jeans, lifted the material and skimmed her fingers along his abs. "The honeymoon is going to be sexy, that's for sure. I won't be able to stop touching my groom."

"Likewise, with my bride." He pushed his hand into the waistband of her leggings and past her panties. He rubbed her in hot little circles, just the way he knew she liked it.

She gasped, and he kissed her, sweet and slow. They hadn't made love since they'd made their baby, and it felt damned good to be together again. The citrus perfume she routinely wore was a welcoming scent. Everything about her worked like an aphrodisiac.

They took turns undressing each other, and he explored the changes in her body. The bump in her tummy was beautifully round, and her breasts were bigger, her nipples and areolas a darker shade of pink.

Jake moved lower, putting his mouth between her legs. He used his tongue, and he didn't stop until she was arching toward him, coming with dizzying pleasure.

"What are you doing to me?" she asked.

"Making you feel good." Making her shake and shiver and tug at the sheets.

In the afterglow, she sat forward, dewy from her orgasm, her body flushed. "I want you inside me."

Heavens, yes. He was already fully aroused from having touched her in such an intimate way. "Climb on top of me."

Carol went for it, straddling him, moaning as she impaled herself, taking him deep. She rode him, stealing his breath from his lungs. He watched her with adoration.

Sleek and warm, she moved up and down, flesh-to-flesh. They clasped hands and looked into each other's eyes. Hers were a shade of green that could've stemmed from the sea.

She was his mermaid. His lady. His future wife.

He said, "We can get married at dusk with a sandcastle as the backdrop, decorated with hundreds of candles, like how it was in the Caribbean."

"I'm so glad I took that trip with you." She leaned forward to kiss him, brushing her lips against his. "What happened between us was meant to be."

And it would be this way forever, he thought. Together they were friends, lovers, parents...

A family in every way.

* * * * *